The Hanged Man of Saint-Pholien

'I love reading Simenon. He makes me think of Chekhov'
William Faulkner

'A truly wonderful writer . . . marvellously readable – lucid, simple, absolutely in tune with the world he creates'
Muriel Spark

'Few writers have ever conveyed with such a sure touch, the bleakness of human life'
A. N. Wilson

'One of the greatest writers of the twentieth century . . . Simenon was unequalled at making us look inside, though the ability was masked by his brilliance at absorbing us obsessively in his stories'
Guardian

'A novelist who entered his fictional world as if he were part of it'
Peter Ackroyd

'The greatest of all, the most genuine novelist we have had in literature'
André Gide

'Superb . . . The most addictive of writers . . . A unique teller of tales'
Observer

'The mysteries of the human personality are revealed in all their disconcerting complexity'
Anita Brookner

'A writer who, more than any other crime novelist, combined high literary reputation with popular appeal'
P. D. James

'A supreme writer . . . Unforgettable vividness'
Independent

'Compelling, remorseless, brilliant'
John Gray

'Extraordinary masterpieces of the twentieth century'
John Banville

ABOUT THE AUTHOR

Georges Simenon was born on 12 February 1903 in Liège, Belgium, and died in 1989 in Lausanne, Switzerland, where he had lived for the latter part of his life. He published seventy-five novels and twenty-eight short stories featuring Inspector Maigret.

The Hanged Man of Saint-Pholien was written in the autumn of 1930 and draws on Simenon's experiences in Liège years earlier, just before he moved to Paris. At that time, he had been involved with a literary set, comprised of poets and young artists. A member of the group, Joseph Jean Kleine, was found hanging from the doorway of the church of Saint-Pholien during this period, a tragedy that left its mark on Simenon.

Penguin is publishing the entire series of Maigret novels.

GEORGES SIMENON

The Hanged Man
of Saint-Pholien

Translated by LINDA COVERDALE

PENGUIN BOOKS

PENGUIN CLASSICS

Published by the Penguin Group
Penguin Books Ltd, 80 Strand, London WC2R ORL, England
Penguin Group (USA) Inc., 375 Hudson Street, New York, New York 10014, USA
Penguin Group (Canada), 90 Eglinton Avenue East, Suite 700, Toronto, Ontario, Canada M4P 2Y3
(a division of Pearson Penguin Canada Inc.)
Penguin Ireland, 25 St Stephen's Green, Dublin 2, Ireland (a division of Penguin Books Ltd)
Penguin Group (Australia), 707 Collins Street, Melbourne, Victoria 3008, Australia
(a division of Pearson Australia Group Pty Ltd)
Penguin Books India Pvt Ltd, 11 Community Centre, Panchsheel Park, New Delhi – 110 017, India
Penguin Group (NZ), 67 Apollo Drive, Rosedale, Auckland 0632, New Zealand
(a division of Pearson New Zealand Ltd)
Penguin Books (South Africa) (Pty) Ltd, Block D, Rosebank Office Park, 181 Jan Smuts Avenue,
Parktown North, Gauteng 2193, South Africa

Penguin Books Ltd, Registered Offices: 80 Strand, London WC2R ORL, England

www.penguin.com

First published in French as *Le Pendu de Saint-Pholien* by Fayard 1931
This translation first published 2014
001

Copyright 1931 by Georges Simenon Limited
Translation © Linda Coverdale, 2014
GEORGES SIMENON ® Simenon.tm
MAIGRET ® Georges Simenon Limited
All rights reserved

The moral rights of the author and translator have been asserted

Typeset in 11/13pt Dante by Palimpsest Book Production Ltd, Falkirk, Stirlingshire
Printed in Great Britain by Clays Ltd, St Ives plc

ISBN: 978–0–141–39345–2

www.greenpenguin.co.uk

Penguin Books is committed to a sustainable
future for our business, our readers and our planet.
This book is made from Forest Stewardship
Council™ certified paper.

1. The Crime of Inspector Maigret

No one noticed what was happening. No one suspected that something serious was taking place in the small station's waiting room, where only six passengers sat dejectedly among odours of coffee, beer and lemonade.

It was five in the afternoon, and night was falling. The lamps had been lighted, but through the windows one could still see both German and Dutch railway and customs officials pacing along the platform, stamping their feet for warmth in the grey dusk.

For Gare de Neuschanz is at the northern tip of Holland, on the German border.

A railway station of no importance. Neuschanz is barely a village. It isn't on any main railway line. A few trains come through mostly in the morning and evening, carrying German workers attracted by the high wages paid in Dutch factories.

And the same ceremony is performed every time: the German train stops at one end of the platform; the Dutch train waits at the other end. The train staff in orange caps and the ones wearing the dull green or Prussian blue uniforms get together to pass the time during the hour allotted for customs formalities.

As there are only twenty or so passengers per train, mostly regular commuters on a first-name basis with the customs men, such formalities do not take long.

The passengers go and sit in the station restaurant, which resembles all those found at international borders. The prices are marked in *cents* and *Pfennige*. A display case contains Dutch chocolate and German cigarettes. Gin and schnapps are served.

That evening, the place felt stuffy. A woman dozed at the cash register. Steam was shooting from the coffee percolator. Through the open kitchen door came the whistling of a wireless as a boy fiddled with its knobs.

A cosy scene, and yet a few small things were enough to insinuate an uneasy sense of mystery and adventure into the atmosphere: the two different national uniforms, for example, and the posters, some advertising German winter sports, others a trade fair in Utrecht.

Off in a corner was a man of about thirty, his face wan and stubbled, in threadbare clothing and a soft felt hat of some vague grey, someone who might well have drifted all around Europe.

He had arrived on the Holland train. When he had produced a ticket for Bremen, the conductor had explained in German that he had chosen a roundabout route without any express trains.

The man had indicated that he did not understand. He had ordered coffee, in French, and everyone had considered him with curiosity.

His eyes were feverish, too deeply sunk in their orbits. He smoked with his cigarette stuck to his lower lip, a small detail that spoke volumes about his weariness or indifference.

At his feet was a small suitcase of the kind sold in any cheap store, made of cardboard treated to look like leather. It was new.

When his coffee arrived, he pulled a handful of loose change from his pocket: French and Belgian tokens, some tiny silver Dutch coins.

The waitress had to select the correct amount herself.

People paid less attention to a traveller sitting at the neighbouring table, a tall, heavy fellow, broad in the shoulders. He wore a thick black overcoat with a velvet collar and a celluloid protector cradled the knot of his necktie.

The first man kept anxiously watching the railway employees through the glass door, as if he feared missing a train.

The second man studied him, calmly, almost implacably, puffing on his pipe.

The nervous traveller left his seat for two minutes to go to the toilet. Without even leaning down, simply by moving a foot, the other man then drew the small suitcase towards him and replaced it with one exactly like it.

Thirty minutes later, the train left. The two men took seats in the same third-class compartment, but without speaking to each other.

At Leer, the other passengers left the train, which still continued along its way for the two remaining travellers.

At ten o'clock it pulled in beneath the monumental glass roof of Bremen Station, where the arc-lamps made everyone's face look deathly pale.

The first traveller must not have known a word of German, because he headed several times in the wrong direction, went into the first-class restaurant and managed only after much coming and going to find the third-class buffet, where he did not sit down. Pointing at some sausages in bread rolls, he gestured to explain that he wished to take them with him and once again paid by holding out a handful of coins.

Carrying his small suitcase, he wandered for more than half an hour through the wide streets near the station, as if he were looking for something.

And when the man with the velvet collar, who was following him patiently, saw him finally turn left and walk quickly into a poorer neighbourhood, he understood that the fellow had simply been seeking an inexpensive hotel.

The younger man's pace was slowing down, and he examined several such establishments suspiciously before choosing a seedy-looking one with a large white globe of frosted glass over the front door.

He was still carrying his suitcase in one hand and his little sausages in bread rolls wrapped in tissue paper in the other.

The street was bustling. Fog began to drift in, dimming the light from the shop windows.

The man with the heavy overcoat finally managed to obtain the room next to that of the first traveller.

A poor room, like all the other poor rooms in the world, except, perhaps, that poverty is nowhere more dispiriting than in northern Germany.

But there was a communicating door between the two rooms, a door with a keyhole.

The second man was thus able to witness the opening of the suitcase, which turned out to contain only old newspapers.

He saw the other fellow turn so white that it was painful to witness, saw him turn the suitcase over and over in his trembling hands, scattering the newspapers around the room.

The rolls and sausages sat on the table, still in their wrapping, but the young man, who had not eaten since four that afternoon, never even gave them a glance.

He rushed back to the station, losing his way, asking for directions ten times, blurting out over and over in such a strong accent that he could barely be understood: 'Bahnhof?'

He was so upset that, to make himself better understood, he imitated the sound of a train!

He reached the station. He wandered in the vast hall, spotted a pile of luggage somewhere and stole up to it like a thief to make sure that his suitcase wasn't there.

And he gave a start whenever someone went by with the same kind of suitcase.

The second man followed him everywhere, keeping a sombre eye on him.

Not until midnight, one following the other, did they return to the hotel.

The keyhole framed the scene: the young man collapsed in a chair, his head in his hands. When he stood up, he snapped his fingers as if both enraged and overcome by his fate.

And that was the end. He pulled a revolver from his pocket, opened his mouth as wide as he could and pressed the trigger.

A moment later there were ten people in the room, although Detective Chief Inspector Maigret, still in his overcoat with its velvet collar, was attempting to keep them out. *Polizei*, they kept saying, and *Mörder*.

The young man was even more pitiful dead than alive.

The soles of his shoes had holes in them, and one leg of his trousers had been pushed up by his fall, revealing an incongruously red sock on a pale, hairy shin.

A policeman arrived and with a few imperious words sent the crowd out on to the landing, except for Maigret, who produced his detective chief inspector's badge of the Police Judiciaire in Paris.

The officer did not speak French. Maigret could venture only a few words of German.

Within ten minutes, a car pulled up outside the hotel, and some officials in civilian clothes rushed in.

Out on the landing, the onlookers now discussed the *Franzose* instead of the *Polizei* and watched the inspector with interest. As if snapping off a light, however, a few orders put an end to their excited speculation, and they returned to their rooms. Down in the street, a silent group of bystanders kept a respectful distance.

Inspector Maigret still clenched his pipe between his teeth, but it had gone out. And his fleshy face, which seemed punched out of dense clay by strong thumbs, bore an expression bordering on fear or disaster.

'I would like permission to conduct my own inquiry while you are conducting yours,' he announced. 'One thing is certain: this man committed suicide. He is a Frenchman.'

'You were following him?'

'It would take too long to explain. I would like your technicians to photograph him from all angles and with as much clarity of detail as possible.'

Commotion had given way to silence in the hotel room; only Maigret and two policemen were left.

One of the Germans, a fresh-faced young man with a

shaved head, wore a morning coat and striped trousers. His official title was something like 'doctor of forensic science', and every now and then he wiped the lenses of his gold-rimmed spectacles.

The other man, equally rosy but less formal in his attire, was rummaging around everywhere and making an effort to speak French.

They found nothing except a passport in the name of Louis Jeunet, mechanic, born in Aubervilliers. As for the revolver, it carried the mark of a firearms manufacturer in Herstal, Belgium.

That night, back at the headquarters of the Police Judiciaire on Quai des Orfèvres, no one would have pictured Maigret, silent and seemingly crushed by the turn of events, watching his German colleagues work, keeping out of the way of the photographers and forensic pathologists, waiting with stubborn concern, his pipe still out, for the pathetic harvest handed over to him at around three in the morning: the dead man's clothes, his passport and a dozen photos taken by magnesium flashlights to hallucinatory effect.

Maigret was not far from – indeed quite close to – thinking that he had just killed a man.

A man he didn't know! He knew nothing about him! There was no proof whatsoever that he was wanted by the law!

It had all begun the previous day in Brussels, in the most unexpected way. Maigret happened to have been sent there to confer with the Belgian police about some Italian refugees who had been expelled from France and whose activities were now cause for concern.

An assignment that had seemed like a pleasure trip! The meetings had taken less time than anticipated, leaving the inspector a few hours to himself.

And simple curiosity had led him to step inside a small café in Rue Montagne aux Herbes Potagères.

It was ten in the morning; the café was practically deserted. While the jovial proprietor was talking his ear off in a friendly way, however, Maigret had noticed a customer at the far end of the room, where the light was dim, who was absorbed in a strange task.

The man was shabby and looked for all the world like one of the chronically unemployed found in every big city, always on the lookout for an opportunity.

Except that he was pulling thousand-franc notes from his pocket and counting them, after which he wrapped them in grey paper, tied the package with string and addressed it. At least thirty notes, 30,000 Belgian francs! Maigret had frowned at that, and when the unknown man left after paying for his coffee, the inspector had followed him to the nearest post office.

There he had managed to read the address over the man's shoulder, an address written in a handwriting much more sophisticated than a simple schoolboy scrawl:

Monsieur Louis Jeunet
18, Rue de la Roquette, Paris

But what struck Maigret the most was the description: *Printed matter.*

Thirty thousand francs travelling as simple newsprint, as ordinary brochures – because the parcel hadn't even been sent via registered mail!

A postal clerk weighed it: 'Seventy centimes . . .'

The sender paid and left. Maigret had noted down the name and address. He then followed his man and had been amused – for a moment – at the thought of making a present of him to the Belgian police. Later on he would go to find the chief commissioner of the Brussels police and casually remark, 'Oh, by the way, while I was having a glass of your delicious gueuze beer, I spotted a crook . . . All you'll have to do is pick him up at such-and-such a place . . .'

Maigret was feeling positively cheerful. A gentle play of autumn sunshine sent warm air wafting through the city.

At eleven o'clock, the unknown man spent thirty-two francs on a suitcase of imitation leather – perhaps even imitation canvas – in a shop in Rue Neuve. And Maigret, playing along, bought the same one, with no thought of what might come next.

At half past eleven, the man turned into a little alley and entered a hotel, the name of which Maigret couldn't manage to see. The man shortly reappeared and at Gare du Nord took the train to Amsterdam.

This time, the inspector hesitated. Was his decision influenced, perhaps, by the feeling that he had already seen that face somewhere?

'It probably isn't anything important. But – what if it is?'

No urgent business awaited him in Paris. At the Dutch border, he had been intrigued by the way the man, with what was clearly practised skill, heaved his suitcase up on to the roof of the train before it stopped at the customs station.

'We'll see what happens when he gets off somewhere . . .'

Except that he did not stay in Amsterdam, where he

simply purchased a third-class ticket for Bremen. Then the train set off across the Dutch plain, with its canals dotted with sailboats that seemed to be gliding along right out in the fields.

Neuschanz . . . Bremen . . .

Just on the off chance, Maigret had managed to switch the suitcases. For hours on end, he had tried without success to classify this fellow with one of the familiar police labels.

'Too nervous for a real international criminal. Or else he's the kind of underling who gets his bosses nabbed . . . A conspirator? Anarchist? He speaks only French, and we've hardly any conspirators in France these days, or even any militant anarchists! Some petty crook off on his own?'

Would a crook have lived so cheaply after mailing off 30,000-franc notes in plain grey paper?

In the stations where there was a long wait, the man drank no alcohol, consuming simply coffee and the occasional roll or brioche.

He was not familiar with the line, because at every station he would ask nervously – even anxiously – if he was going in the right direction.

Although he was not a strong, burly man, his hands bore the signs of manual labour. His nails were black, and too long as well, which suggested that he had not worked for a while.

His complexion indicated anaemia, perhaps destitution. And Maigret gradually forgot the clever joke he'd thought of playing on the Belgian police by jauntily presenting them with a trussed-up crook.

This conundrum fascinated him. He kept finding excuses for his behaviour.

'Amsterdam isn't that far from Paris . . .'

And then . . .

'So what! I can take an express from Bremen and be back in thirteen hours.'

The man was dead. There was no compromising paper on him, nothing to reveal what he had been doing except an ordinary revolver of the most popular make in Europe.

He seemed to have killed himself only because someone had stolen his suitcase! Otherwise, why would he have bought rolls from the station buffet but never eaten them? And why spend a day travelling, when he might have stayed in Brussels and blown his brains out just as easily as in a German hotel?

Still, there was the suitcase, which might hold the solution to this puzzle. And that's why – after the naked body had been photographed and examined from head to toe, carried out wrapped in a sheet, hoisted into a police van and driven away – the inspector shut himself up in his hotel room.

He looked haggard. Although he filled his pipe as always, tapping gently with his thumb, he was only trying to persuade himself that he felt calm.

The dead man's thin, drawn face was haunting him. He kept seeing him snapping his fingers, then immediately opening his mouth wide for the gunshot.

Maigret felt so troubled – indeed, almost remorseful – that only after painful hesitation did he reach for the suitcase.

And yet that suitcase would supposedly prove him right! Wasn't he going to find there evidence that the man he was weak enough to pity was a crook, a dangerous criminal, perhaps a murderer?

The keys still hung from a string tied to the handle, as they had in the shop in Rue Neuve. Maigret opened the suitcase and first took out a dark-grey suit, less threadbare than the one the dead man had been wearing. Beneath the suit were two dirty shirts frayed at the collar and cuffs, rolled into a ball, and a detachable collar with thin pink stripes that had been worn for at least two weeks, because it was quite soiled wherever it had touched the wearer's neck . . . Soiled and shoddy . . .

That was all. Except for the bottom of the suitcase: green paper lining, two brand-new straps with buckles and swiveling tabs that hadn't been used.

Maigret shook out the clothing, checked the pockets. Empty! Seized with a choking sense of anguish, he kept looking, driven by his desire – his need – to find something.

Hadn't a man killed himself because someone had stolen this suitcase? And there was nothing in it but an old suit and some dirty laundry!

Not even a piece of paper. Nothing in the way of documents. No sign of any clue to the dead man's past.

The hotel room was decorated with new, inexpensive and aggressively floral wallpaper in garish colours. The furniture, however, was old and rickety, broken-down, and the printed calico draped over the table was too filthy to touch.

The street was deserted, the shutters of the shops were closed, but a hundred metres away there was the reassuring thrum of steady traffic at a crossroads.

Maigret looked at the communicating door, at the keyhole he no longer dared to peek through. He remembered that the technicians had chalked the outline of the body on the floor of the neighbouring room for future study.

Carrying the dead man's suit, still wrinkled from the suitcase, he went next door on tiptoe so as not to awaken other guests, and perhaps because he felt burdened by this mystery.

The outline on the floor was contorted, but accurately drawn.

When Maigret tried to fit the jacket, waistcoat and trousers into the outline, his eyes lit up, and he bit down hard on his pipe-stem. The clothing was at least three sizes too large: it did not belong to the dead man.

What the tramp had been keeping so protectively in his suitcase, a thing so precious to him that he'd killed himself when it was lost, was someone else's suit!

2. Monsieur Van Damme

The Bremen newspapers simply announced in a few lines that a Frenchman named Louis Jeunet, a mechanic, had committed suicide in a hotel in the city and that poverty seemed to have been the motive for his act.

But by the time those lines appeared the following morning, that information was no longer correct. In fact, while leafing through Jeunet's passport, Maigret had noticed an interesting detail: on the sixth page, in the column listing *age*, *height*, *hair*, *forehead*, *eyebrows* and so on for the bearer's description, the word *forehead* appeared before *hair* instead of after it.

It so happened that six months earlier, the Paris Sûreté had discovered in Saint-Ouen a veritable factory for fake passports, military records, foreign residence permits and other official documents, a certain number of which they had seized. The counterfeiters themselves had admitted, however, that hundreds of their forgeries had been in circulation for several years and that, because they had kept no records, they could not provide a list of their customers.

The passport proved that Louis Jeunet had been one of them, which meant that his name was not Louis Jeunet.

And so, the single more or less solid fact in this inquiry had melted away. The man who had killed himself that night was now a complete unknown.

★

Having been granted all the authorization he needed, at nine o'clock the next morning Maigret arrived at the morgue, which the general public was free to visit after it opened its doors for the day.

He searched in vain for a dark corner from which to keep watch, although he really didn't expect much in the way of results. The morgue was a modern building, like most of the city and all its public buildings, and it was even more sinister than the ancient morgue in Quai de l'Horloge, in Paris. More sinister precisely because of its sharp, clean lines and perspectives, the uniform white of the walls, which reflected a harsh light, and the refrigeration units as shiny as machines in a power station. The place looked like a model factory: one where the raw material was human bodies.

The man who had called himself Louis Jeunet was there, less disfigured than might have been expected, because specialists had partially reconstructed his face. There were also a young woman and a drowned fellow who'd been fished from the harbour.

Brimming with health and tightly buttoned into his spotless uniform, the guard looked like a museum attendant.

In the space of an hour, surprisingly enough, some thirty people passed through the viewing hall. When one woman asked to see a body that was not on display, electric bells rang and numbers were barked into a telephone.

In an area on the first floor, one of the drawers in a vast cabinet filling an entire wall glided out into a freight lift, and a few moments later a steel box emerged on the ground floor just as books in some libraries are delivered to reading rooms.

It was the body that had been requested. The woman

bent over it – and was led away, sobbing, to an office at the far end of the hall, where a young clerk took down her statement.

Few people took any interest in Louis Jeunet. Shortly after ten o'clock, however, a smartly attired man arrived in a private car, entered the hall, looked around for the suicide and examined him carefully.

Maigret was not far away. He drew closer and, after studying the visitor, decided that he didn't look German.

As soon as this visitor noticed Maigret approaching, moreover, he started uneasily, and must have come to the same conclusion as Maigret had about him.

'Are you French?' he asked bluntly.

'Yes. You, too?'

'Actually, I'm Belgian, but I've been living in Bremen for a few years now.'

'And you knew a man named Jeunet?'

'No! I . . . I read in this morning's paper that a French-man had committed suicide in Bremen . . . I lived in Paris for a long time . . . and I felt curious enough to come and take a look.'

Maigret was completely calm, as he always was in such moments, when his face would settle into an expression of such stubborn density that he seemed even a touch bovine.

'Are you with the police?'

'Yes! The Police Judiciaire.'

'So you've come up here because of this case? Oh, wait: that's impossible, the suicide only happened last night . . . Tell me, do you have any French acquaintances in Bremen? No? In that case, if I can assist you in any way . . . May I offer you an aperitif?'

Shortly afterwards, Maigret followed the other man outside and joined him in his car, which the Belgian drove himself.

And as he drove he chattered away, a perfect example of the enthusiastic, energetic businessman. He seemed to know everyone, greeted passers-by, pointed out buildings, provided a running commentary.

'Here you have Norddeutscher Lloyd . . . Have you heard about the new liner they've launched? They're clients of mine . . .'

He waved towards a building in which almost every window displayed the name of a different firm.

'On the fifth floor, to the left, you can see my office.'

Porcelain sign letters on the window spelled out: *Joseph Van Damme, Import-Export Commission Agent.*

'Would you believe that sometimes I go a month without having a chance to speak French? My employees and even my secretary are German. That's business for you!'

It would have been hard to divine a single one of Maigret's thoughts from his expression; he seemed a man devoid of subtlety. He agreed; he approved. He admired what he was asked to admire, including the car and its patented suspension system, proudly praised by Van Damme.

The inspector followed his host into a large brasserie teeming with businessmen talking loudly over the tireless efforts of a Viennese orchestra and the clinking of beer mugs.

'You'd never guess how much this clientele is worth in millions!' crowed the Belgian. 'Listen! You don't understand German? Well, our neighbour here is busy selling a cargo of wool currently on its way to Europe from

Australia; he has thirty or forty ships in his fleet, and I could show you others like him. So, what'll you have? Personally, I recommend the Pilsner. By the way . . .'

Maigret's face showed no trace of a smile at the transition.

'By the way, what do you think about this suicide? A poor man down on his luck, as the papers here are saying?'

'It's possible.'

'Are you looking into it?'

'No: that's a matter for the German police. And as it's a clear case of suicide . . .'

'Oh, obviously! Of course, the thing that struck me was only that he was French, because we get so few of them up in the North!'

He rose to go and shake the hand of a man who was on his way out, then hurried back.

'Please excuse me – he runs a big insurance company, he's worth a hundred million . . . But listen, inspector: it's almost noon, you must come and have lunch with me! I'm not married, so I can only invite you to a restaurant, and you won't eat as you would in Paris, but I'll do my best to see that you don't do too badly. So, that's settled, right?'

He summoned the waiter, paid the bill. And when he pulled his wallet from his pocket, he did something that Maigret had often seen when businessmen like him had their aperitifs in bars around the Paris stock exchange, for they had that inimitable way of leaning backwards, throwing out their chests while tucking in their chins and opening with careless satisfaction that sacred object: the leather *portefeuille* plump with money.

'Let's go!'

★

Van Damme hung on to the inspector until almost five o'clock, after sweeping him along to his office – three clerks and a typist – but by then he'd made him promise that if he did not leave Bremen that evening, they would spend it together at a well-known cabaret.

Maigret found himself back in the crowd, alone with his thoughts, although they were in considerable disarray. Strictly speaking, were they even really thoughts?

His mind was comparing two figures, two men, and trying to establish a relationship between them.

Because there was one! Van Damme hadn't gone to the trouble of driving to the morgue simply to look at the dead body of a stranger. And the pleasure of speaking French was not the only reason he had invited Maigret to lunch. Besides, he had gradually revealed his true personality only after becoming increasingly persuaded that his companion had no interest in the case. And perhaps not much in the way of brains, either!

That morning, Van Damme had been worried. His smile had seemed forced. By the end of the afternoon, on the other hand, he had resurfaced as a sharp little operator, always on the go, busy, chatty, enthusiastic, mixing with financial big shots, driving his car, on the phone, rattling off instructions to his typist and hosting expensive dinners, proud and happy to be what he was.

And the second man was an anaemic tramp with grubby clothes and worn-out shoes, who had bought some sausages in rolls without the faintest idea that he would never get to eat them!

Van Damme must have already found himself another companion for the evening aperitif, in the same atmosphere of Viennese music and beer.

At six o'clock, a cover would close quietly on a metal bin, shutting away the naked body of the false Louis Jeunet, and the lift would deliver it to the freezer to spend the night in a numbered compartment.

Maigret went along to the Polizeipräsidium. Some officers were exercising, stripped to the waist in spite of the chill, in a courtyard with vivid red walls.

In the laboratory, a young man with a faraway look in his eye was waiting for him near a table on which all the dead man's possessions had been laid out and neatly labelled.

The man spoke perfect textbook French and took pride in coming up with *le mot juste*.

Beginning with the nondescript grey suit Jeunet had been wearing when he died, he explained that all the linings had been unpicked, every seam examined, and that nothing had been found.

'The suit comes from La Belle Jardinière in Paris. The material is fifty per cent cotton, so it is a cheap garment. We noticed some grease spots, including stains of mineral jelly, which suggest that the man worked in or was often inside a factory, workshop or garage. There are no labels or laundry marks in his linen. The shoes were purchased in Rheims. Same as the clothing: mass-produced, of mediocre quality. The socks are of cotton, the kind peddled in the street at four or five francs a pair. They have holes in them but have never been mended.

'All these clothes have been placed in a strong paper bag and shaken, and the dust obtained was analysed.

'We were thus able to confirm the provenance of those grease stains. The clothes are in fact impregnated with a fine metallic powder found only on the belongings of fitters, metal-workers, and, in general, those who labour in machine shops.

'These elements are absent from the items I will call clothing B, items which have not been worn for at least six years.

'One more difference: in the pockets of suit A we found traces of French government-issue tobacco, what you call shag tobacco. In the pockets of clothing B, however, there were particles of yellowish imitation Egyptian tobacco.

'But now I come to the most important point. The spots found on clothing B are not grease spots. They are old human bloodstains, probably from arterial blood.

'The material has not been washed for years. The man who wore this suit must have been literally drenched in blood. And finally, certain tears suggest that there may have been a struggle, because in various places, for example on the lapels, the weave of the cloth has been torn as if it had been clawed by fingernails.

'The items of clothing B have labels from the tailor Roger Morcel, Rue Haute-Sauvenière, in Liège.

'As for the revolver, it's a model that was discontinued two years ago.

'If you wish to leave me your address, I will send you a copy of the report I'll be drawing up for my superiors.'

By eight that evening, Maigret had finished with the formalities. The German police had handed the dead man's clothes over to him along with the ones in the suitcase, which the technician had referred to as clothing B. And it had been decided that, until further notice, the body would be kept at the disposition of the French authorities in the mortuary refrigerator unit.

Maigret had a copy of Joseph Van Damme's public record: born in Liège of Flemish parents; travelling salesman, then director of a commission agency bearing his name.

He was thirty-two. A bachelor. He had lived in Bremen for only three years and, after some initial difficulties, now seemed to be doing nicely.

The inspector returned to his hotel room, where he sat for a long time on the edge of his bed with the two cheap suitcases in front of him. He had opened the communicating door to the neighbouring room, where nothing had been touched since the previous day, and he was struck by how little disorder the tragedy had left behind. In one place on the wallpaper, beneath a pink flower, was a very small brown spot, the only bloodstain. On the table lay the two sausage bread rolls, still wrapped in paper. A fly was sitting on them.

That morning, Maigret had sent two photos of the dead man to Paris and asked that the Police Judiciaire publish them in as many newspapers as possible.

Should the search begin there? In Paris, where the police at least had an address, the one where Jeunet had sent himself the thirty thousand-franc notes from Brussels?

Or in Liège, where clothing B had been bought a few years before? In Rheims, where the dead man's shoes had come from? In Brussels, where Jeunet had wrapped up his package of 30,000 francs? Bremen, where he had died and where a certain Joseph Van Damme had come to take a look at his corpse, denying all the while that he had ever known him?

The hotel manager appeared, made a long speech in German and, as far as the inspector could tell, asked him if the room where the tragedy had taken place could be cleaned and rented out.

Maigret grunted his assent, washed his hands, paid and went off with his two suitcases, their obviously poor quality in stark contrast with his comfortably bourgeois appearance.

There was no clear reason to tackle his investigation from one angle or another. And if he chose Paris, it was above all because of the strikingly foreign atmosphere all around him that constantly disturbed his habits, his way of thinking and, in the end, depressed him.

The local tobacco – rather yellow and too mild – had even killed his desire to smoke!

He slept in the express, waking at the Belgian border as day was breaking, and passed through Liège thirty minutes later. He stood at the door of the carriage to stare half-heartedly out at the station, where the train halted for only thirty minutes, not enough time for a visit to Rue Haute-Sauvenière.

At two that afternoon he arrived at Gare du Nord and plunged into the Parisian crowds, where his first concern was to visit a tobacconist.

He was groping around in his pockets for some French coins when someone jostled him. The two suitcases were sitting at his feet. When he bent to retrieve them, he could find only one, and looking around in vain for the other, he realized that there was no point in alerting the police.

One detail, in any case, reassured him. The remaining suitcase had its two keys tied to the handle with a small string. That was the suitcase containing the clothing.

The thief had carried off the one full of old newspapers.

Had he been simply a thief, the kind that prowl through stations? In which case, wasn't it odd that he'd stolen such a crummy-looking piece of luggage?

Maigret settled into a taxi, savouring both his pipe and the familiar hubbub of the streets. Passing a kiosk, he caught a glimpse of a front-page photograph and even at a distance recognized one of the pictures of Louis Jeunet he had sent from Bremen.

He considered stopping by his home on Boulevard Richard-Lenoir to kiss his wife and change his clothes, but the incident at the station was bothering him.

'If the thief really was after the second suit of clothes, then how was he informed in Paris that I was carrying them and would arrive precisely when I did?'

It was as if fresh mysteries now hovered around the pale face and thin form of the tramp of Neuschanz and Bremen: shadowy forms were shifting, as on a photographic plate plunged into a developing bath.

And they would have to become clearer, revealing faces, names, thoughts and feelings, entire lives.

For the moment, in the centre of that plate lay only a naked body, and a harsh light shone on the face German doctors had done their fumbling best to make look human again.

The shadows? First, a man in Paris who was making off with the suitcase at that very moment. Plus another man who – from Bremen or elsewhere – had sent him instructions. The convivial Joseph Van Damme, perhaps? Or perhaps not! And then there was the person who, years ago, had worn clothing B . . . and the one who, during the struggle, had bled all over him. And the person who had supplied the 30,000 francs to 'Louis Jeunet' – or the person from whom they had been stolen!

It was sunny; the café terraces, heated by braziers, were thronged with people. Drivers were hailing one another. Swarms of people were pushing their way on to buses and trams.

From among all this seething humanity, here and in Bremen, Brussels, Rheims and still other places, the hunt would have to track down two, three, four, five individuals . . .

Fewer, perhaps? Or maybe more . . .

Maigret looked up fondly at the austere façade of police headquarters as he crossed the front courtyard carrying the small suitcase. He greeted the office boy by his first name.

'Did you get my telegram? Did you light a stove?'

'There's a lady here, about the picture! She's in the waiting room, been there for two hours now.'

Maigret did not stop to take off his hat and coat. He didn't even set down the suitcase.

The waiting room, at the end of the corridor lined with the chief inspectors' offices, is almost completely glassed-in and furnished with a few chairs upholstered in green velvet; its sole brick wall displays the list of policemen killed while on special duty.

On one of the chairs sat a woman who was still young, dressed with the humble care that bespeaks long hours of sewing by lamplight, making do with the best one has.

Her black cloth coat had a very thin fur collar. Her hands, in their grey cotton gloves, clutched a handbag made, like Maigret's suitcase, of imitation leather.

Did the inspector notice a vague resemblance between his visitor and the dead man?

Not a facial resemblance, no, but a similarity of expression, of social *class*, so to speak.

She, too, had the washed-out, weary eyes of those whose courage has abandoned them. Her nostrils were pinched and her complexion unhealthily dull.

She had been waiting for two hours and naturally hadn't dared change seats or even move at all. She looked at Maigret through the glass with no hope that he might at last be the person she needed to see.

He opened the door.

'If you would care to follow me to my office, madame.'

When he ushered her in ahead of him she appeared astonished at his courtesy and hesitated, as if confused, in the middle of the room. Along with her handbag she carried a rumpled newspaper showing part of Jeunet's photograph.

'I'm told you know the man who—'

But before he could finish she bit her lips and buried her face in her hands. Almost overcome by a sob she could not control, she moaned, 'He's my husband, monsieur.'

Hiding his feeling, Maigret turned away, then rolled a heavy armchair over for her.

3. The Herbalist's Shop in Rue Picpus

'Did he suffer much?' she asked, as soon as she could speak again.

'No, madame. I can assure you that death was instantaneous.'

She looked at the newspaper in her hand. The words were hard to say.

'In the mouth?'

When the inspector simply nodded, she stared down at the floor, suddenly calm, and as if speaking about a mischievous child she said solemnly, 'He always had to be different from everyone else . . .'

She spoke not as a lover, or even a wife. Although she was not yet thirty, she had a maternal tenderness about her, and the gentle resignation of a nun.

The poor are used to stifling any expression of their despair, because they must get on with life, with work, with the demands made of them day after day, hour after hour. She wiped her eyes with her handkerchief, and her slightly reddened nose erased any prettiness she possessed.

The corners of her mouth kept drooping sadly though she tried to smile as she looked at Maigret.

'Would you mind if I asked you a few questions?' he said, sitting down at his desk. 'Was your husband's name indeed Louis Jeunet? And . . . when did he leave you for the last time?'

Tears sprang to her eyes; she almost began weeping again. Her fingers had balled the handkerchief into a hard little wad.

'Two years ago . . . But I saw him again, once, peering in at the shop window. If my mother hadn't been there . . .'

Maigret realized that he need simply let her talk. Because she would, as much for herself as for him.

'You want to know all about our life, isn't that right? It's the only way to understand why Louis did that . . . My father was a male nurse in Beaujon. He had set up a small herbalist's shop in Rue Picpus, which my mother managed.

'My father died six years ago, and Mama and I have kept up the business.

'I met Louis . . .'

'That was six years ago, did you say?' Maigret asked her. 'Was he already calling himself Jeunet?'

'Yes!' she replied, in some astonishment. 'He was a milling machine operator in a workshop in Belleville . . . He earned a good living . . . I don't know why things happened so quickly, you can't imagine – he was in a hurry about everything, as if some fever were eating at him.

'I'd been seeing him for barely a month when we got married, and he came to live with us. The living quarters behind the shop are too small for three people; we rented a room for Mama over in Rue du Chemin-Vert. She let me have the shop, but as she hadn't saved enough to live on, we gave her 200 francs every month.

'We were happy, I swear to you! Louis would go off to work in the morning; my mother would come to keep me company. He stayed home in the evenings.

'I don't know how to explain this to you, but – I always felt that something was wrong!

'I mean, for example . . . it was as if Louis didn't belong to our world, as if the way we lived was sometimes too much for him.

'He was very sweet to me . . .'

Her expression became wistful; she was almost beautiful when she confessed, 'I don't think many men are like this: he would take me suddenly in his arms, looking so deeply into my eyes that it hurt. Then sometimes, out of the blue, he would push me away – I've never seen such a thing from anyone else – and he'd sigh to himself, "Yet I really am fond of you, my little Jeanne . . ."

'Then it was over. He'd keep busy with this or that without giving me another glance, spend hours repairing a piece of furniture, making me something handy for housework, or fixing a clock.

'My mother didn't much care for him, precisely because she understood that he wasn't like other people.'

'Among his belongings, weren't there some items he guarded with particular care?'

'How did you know?'

She started, a touch frightened, and blurted out, 'An old suit! Once he came home when I'd taken it from a cardboard box on top of the wardrobe and was brushing it. The suit would have been still good enough to wear around the house. I was even going to mend the tears. Louis grabbed it from me, he was furious, shouting cruel things, and that evening – you'd have sworn he hated me!

'We'd been married for a month. After that . . .'

She sighed and looked at Maigret as if in apology for having nothing more for him than this poor story.

'He became more and more strange?'

'It isn't his fault, I'm sure of that! I think he was ill, he worried so . . . We were often in the kitchen, and whenever we'd been happy for a little while, I used to see him change suddenly: he'd stop speaking, look at things – and me – with a nasty smile, and go and throw himself down on his bed without saying goodnight to me.'

'He had no friends?'

'No! No one ever came to see him.'

'He never travelled, received any letters?'

'No. And he didn't like having people in our home. Once in a while, a neighbour who had no sewing machine would come over to use mine, and that was guaranteed to enrage Louis. But he didn't become angry like everyone else, it was something shut up inside . . . and he was the one who seemed to suffer!

'When I told him we were going to have a child, he stared at me like a madman . . .

'That was when he started to drink, fits of it, binges, especially after the baby was born. And yet I know that he loved that child! Sometimes he used to gaze at him in adoration, the way he did with me at first . . .

'The next day, he'd come home drunk, lie down, lock the bedroom door and spend hours in there, whole days.

'The first few times, he'd cry and beg me to forgive him. Maybe if Mama hadn't interfered I might have managed to keep him, but my mother tried to lecture him, and there were awful arguments. Especially when Louis went two or three days without going to work!

'Towards the end, we were desperately unhappy. You know what it's like, don't you? His temper got worse and worse. My mother threw him out twice, to remind him that he wasn't the lord and master there.

'But I just know that it wasn't his fault! Something was pushing him, driving him! He would still look at me, or our son, in that old way I told you about . . .

'Only now not so often, and it didn't last long. The final quarrel was dreadful. Mama was there. Louis had helped himself to some money from the shop, and she called him a thief. He went so pale, his eyes all red, as on his bad days, and a crazed look in those eyes . . .

'I can still see him coming closer as if to strangle me! I was terrified and screamed, "Louis!"

'He left, slamming the door so hard the glass shattered.

'That was two years ago. Some neighbourhood women saw him around now and again . . . I went to that factory in Belleville, but they told me he didn't work there any more.

'Someone saw him, though, in a small workshop in Rue de la Roquette where they make beer pumps.

'Me, I saw him once more, maybe six months ago now, through the shop window. Mama is living with me and the child again, and she was in the shop . . . she kept me from running to the door.

'You swear to me that he didn't suffer? That he died instantly? He was an unhappy, unfortunate man, don't you see? You must have understood that by now . . .'

She had relived her story with such intensity, and her husband had had such a strong hold on her, that, without realizing it, she had been reflecting all the feelings she was describing on her own face.

As in his first impression, Maigret was struck by an

unnerving resemblance between this woman and the man in Bremen who had snapped his fingers before shooting a bullet into his mouth.

What's more, that raging fever she had just evoked seemed to have infected her. She fell silent, but all her nerves remained on edge, and she almost gasped for breath. She was waiting for something, she didn't know what.

'He never spoke to you about his past, his childhood?'

'No. He didn't talk much. I only know that he was born in Aubervilliers. And I've always thought he was educated beyond his station in life; he had lovely handwriting, and he knew the Latin names of all the plants. When the woman from the haberdashery next door had a difficult letter to write, he was the one she came to.'

'And you never saw his family?'

'Before we were married, he told me he was an orphan. Chief inspector, there's one more thing I'd like to ask you. Will he be brought back to France?'

When Maigret hesitated to reply, she turned her face away to hide her embarrassment.

'Now the shop belongs to my mother. And the money, too. I know she won't want to pay anything to bring the body home – or give me enough to go and see him! Would it be possible, in this case . . .'

The words died in her throat, and she quickly bent down to retrieve her handkerchief, which had fallen to the floor.

'I will see to it that your husband is brought home, madame.'

She gave him a touching smile, then wiped a tear from her cheek.

'You've understood, I can tell! You feel the same way

I do, chief inspector! It wasn't his fault . . . He was an unhappy man . . .'

'Did he ever have any large sums of money?'

'Only his wages. In the beginning, he gave everything to me. Later on, when he began drinking . . .'

Another faint smile, very sad, and yet full of pity.

She left somewhat calmer, gathering the skimpy fur collar tightly round her neck with her right hand, still clutching the handbag and the tightly folded newspaper in the other.

Maigret found a seedy-looking hotel at 18, Rue de la Roquette, right where it joins Rue de Lappe, with its accordion-band dance halls and squalid housing. That stretch of Roquette is a good fifty metres from Place de la Bastille. Every ground floor hosts a bistro, every house a hotel frequented by drifters, immigrants, tarts and the chronically unemployed.

Tucked away within these vaguely sinister haunts of the underclass, however, are a few workshops, their doors wide open to the street, where men wield hammers and blow-torches amid a constant traffic of heavy trucks.

The contrast is striking: these steady workers, busy employees with waybills in hand, and the sordid or inso-lent creatures who hang around everywhere.

'Jeunet!' rumbled the inspector, pushing open the door of the hotel office on the ground floor.

'Not here!'

'He's still got his room?'

He'd been spotted for a policeman, and got a reluctant reply.

'Yes, room 19!'

'By the week? The month?'

'The month!'

'You have any mail for him?'

The manager turned evasive, but in the end handed over to Maigret the package Jeunet had sent himself from Brussels.

'Did he receive many like this?'

'A few times . . .'

'Never any letters?'

'No! Maybe he got three packages, in all. A quiet man. I don't see why the police should want to come bothering him.'

'He worked?'

'At number 65, down the street.'

'Regularly?'

'Depended. Some weeks yes, others, no.'

Maigret demanded the key to the room. He found nothing there, however, except a ruined pair of shoes with flapping soles, an empty tube of aspirin and some mechanic's overalls tossed into a corner.

Back downstairs, he questioned the manager again, learning that Louis Jeunet saw no one, did not go out with women and basically led a humdrum life, aside from a few trips lasting three or four days.

But no one stays in one of these hotels, in this neighbourhood, unless there's something wrong somewhere, and the manager knew that as well as Maigret.

'It's not what you think,' he admitted grudgingly. 'With him, it's the bottle! And how – in binges. Novenas, my wife and I call them. Buckle down for three weeks, go off to work every day, then . . . for a while he'd drink until he passed out on his bed.'

'You never saw anything suspicious about his behaviour?'

But the man shrugged, as if to say that in his hotel everyone who walked through the door looked suspicious.

At number 65, in a huge workshop open to the street, they made machines to draw off beer. Maigret was met by a foreman, who had already seen Jeunet's picture in the paper.

'I was just going to write to the police!' he exclaimed. 'He was still working here last week. A fellow who earned eight francs fifty an hour!'

'When he was working.'

'Ah, you already know? When he was working, true! There are lots of them like that, but in general those others regularly take one drink too many, or they splurge on a champion hangover every Saturday. Him, it was sudden-like, no warning: he'd drink for a solid week. Once, when we had a rush job, I went to his hotel room. Well! There he was, all alone, drinking right out of a bottle set on the floor by his bed. A sorry sight, I swear.'

In Aubervilliers, nothing. The registry office held a single record of one Louis Jeunet, son of Gaston Jeunet, day labourer, and Berthe Marie Dufoin, domestic servant. Gaston Jeunet had died ten years earlier; his wife had moved away.

As for Louis Jeunet, no one knew anything about him, except that six years before he had written from Paris to request a copy of his birth certificate.

But the passport was still a forgery, which meant that the man who had killed himself in Bremen – after marrying the herbalist woman in Rue Picpus and having a son – was not the real Jeunet.

The criminal records in the Préfecture were another dead end: nothing indexed under the name of Jeunet, no finger-prints matching the ones of the dead man, taken in Germany. Evidently this desperate soul had never run afoul of the law in France or abroad, because headquarters kept tabs on the police records of most European nations.

The records went back only six years. At which point, there was a Louis Jeunet, a drilling machine operator, who had a job and lived the life of a decent working man.

He married. He already owned clothing B, which had provoked the first scene with his wife and years later would prove the cause of his death.

He had no friends, received no mail. He appeared to know Latin and therefore to have received an above-average education.

Back in his office, Maigret drew up a request for the German police to release the body, disposed of a few current matters and, with a sullen, sour face, once again opened the yellow suitcase, the contents of which had been so carefully labelled by the technician in Bremen.

To this he added the package of thirty Belgian thousand-franc notes – but abruptly decided to snap the string and copy down the serial numbers on the bills, a list he sent off to the police in Brussels, asking that they be traced.

He did all this with studied concentration, as if he were trying to convince himself that he was doing something useful.

From time to time, however, he would glance with a kind of bitterness at the crime-scene photos spread out on his desk, and his pen would hover in mid-air as he chewed on the stem of his pipe.

Regretfully, he was about to set the investigation aside and leave for home when he learned that he had a telephone call from Rheims.

It was about the picture published in the papers. The proprietor of the Café de Paris, in Rue Carnot, claimed to have seen the man in question in his establishment six days earlier – and had remembered this because the man got so drunk that he had finally stopped serving him.

Maigret hesitated. The dead man's shoes had come from Rheims – which had now cropped up again.

Moreover, these worn-out shoes had been bought months earlier, so Louis Jeunet had not just happened to be in Rheims by accident.

One hour later, the inspector took his seat on the Rheims express, arriving there at ten o'clock. A fashionable establishment favoured by the bourgeoisie, the Café de Paris was crowded that evening; three games of billiards were in full swing, and people at a few tables were playing cards.

It was a traditional café of the French provinces, where customers shake hands with the cashier and waiters know all the regulars by name: local notables, commercial travellers and so forth. It even had the traditional round nickel-plated receptacles for the café dishcloths.

'I am the inspector whom you telephoned earlier this evening.'

Standing by the counter, the proprietor was keeping an eye on his staff while he dispensed advice to the billiard players.

'Ah, yes! Well, I've already told you all I know.'

Somewhat embarrassed, he spoke in a low voice.

'Let me think . . . He was sitting over in that corner, near the third billiard table, and he ordered a brandy, then another, and a third . . . It was at about this same time of night. People were giving him funny looks because – how shall I put this? – he wasn't exactly our usual class of customer.'

'Did he have any luggage?'

'An old suitcase with a broken lock. I remember that when he left, the suitcase fell open and some old clothes spilled out. He even asked me for some string to tie it closed.'

'Did he speak to anyone?'

The proprietor glanced over at one of the billiard players, a tall, thin young man, a snappy dresser, the very picture of a sharp player whose every bank shot would be studied with respect.

'Not exactly . . . Won't you have something, inspector? We could sit over here, look!'

He chose a table with trays stacked on it, off to one side.

'By about midnight, he was as white as this marble tabletop. He'd had maybe eight or nine brandies. And I didn't like that stare he had – it takes some people that way, the alcohol. They don't get agitated or start rambling on, but at some point they simply pass out cold. Everyone had noticed him. I went over to tell him that I couldn't serve him any more, and he didn't protest in any way.'

'Was anyone still playing billiards?'

'The fellows you see over at that third table. Regulars, here every evening: they have a club, organize competitions. Well, the man left – and that's when there was that business with the suitcase falling open. The state he was in, I don't know how he managed to tie the string. I closed up a half-hour later. These gentlemen here shook my hand leaving, and I remember one of them said, 'We'll find him off somewhere in the gutter!'

The proprietor glanced again at the smartly dressed player with the white, well-manicured hands, the impeccable tie, the polished shoes that creaked each time he moved around the billiard table.

'I might as well tell you everything, especially since it's probably some fluke or a misunderstanding . . . The next day, a travelling salesman who drops by every month and who was here that night, well, he told me that at about one in the morning he'd seen the drunk and Monsieur Belloir walking along together. He even saw them both go into Monsieur Belloir's house!'

'That's the tall blond fellow?'

'Yes. He lives five minutes from here, in a handsome house in Rue de Vesle. He's the deputy director of the Banque de Crédit.'

'Is the salesman here tonight?'

'No, he's off on his regular tour through his eastern territories, won't be back until mid-November or so. I told him he must have been mistaken, but he stuck to his story. I almost mentioned it to Monsieur Belloir, as a little joke, but thought, better not. He might have been offended, right? In fact, I'd appreciate it if you wouldn't make a big deal out of what I just told you – or at least don't make it look as if it came from me. In my profession . . .'

Having just scored a break of forty-eight points, the player in question was looking around to gauge everyone's reaction while he rubbed the tip of his cue with green chalk. He frowned almost imperceptibly when he noticed Maigret sitting with the proprietor.

For, like most people trying to appear relaxed, the café owner looked worried, as if he were up to something.

Belloir called out to him from across the room.

'It's your turn, Monsieur Émile!'

4. The Unexpected Visitor

The house was new, and there was something in the studied refinement of its design and building materials that created a feeling of comfort, of crisp, confident modernism and a well-established fortune.

Red bricks, freshly repointed; natural stone; a front door of varnished oak, with brass fittings.

It was only 8.30 in the morning when Maigret turned up at that door, half hoping to catch a candid glimpse of the Belloir family's private life.

The façade, in any case, seemed suitable for a bank deputy director, an impression increased by the immaculately turned-out maid who opened the door. The entrance hall was quite large, with a door of bevelled glass panes at the end. The walls were of faux marble, and geometric patterns in two colours embellished the granite floor.

To the left, two sets of double doors of pale oak, leading to the drawing room and dining room.

Among the clothes hanging from a portmanteau was a coat for a child of four or five. A big-bellied umbrella stand held a Malacca cane with a gold pommel.

Maigret had only a moment to absorb this atmosphere of flawless domesticity, for he had barely mentioned Monsieur Belloir when the maid replied, 'If you'd be so good as to follow me, *the gentlemen* are expecting you.'

She walked towards the glass-paned door. Passing

another, half-open door, the inspector caught a glimpse of the dining room, cosy and neat, where a young woman in a peignoir and a little boy of four were having their breakfast at a nicely laid table.

Beyond the last door was a staircase of pale wooden panelling with a red floral carpet runner fixed to each step by a brass rod.

A large green plant sat on the landing. The maid was already turning the knob of another door, to a study, where three men turned as one towards their visitor.

There was a reaction of shock, deep unease, even real distress that froze the looks in their eyes, which only the maid never noticed as she asked in a perfectly natural voice, 'Would you like me to take your coat?'

One of the three gentlemen was Belloir, perfectly dressed, with not a blond hair out of place. The man next to him was a little more casually attired, and a stranger to Maigret. The third man, however, was none other than Joseph Van Damme, the businessman from Bremen.

Two of the men spoke simultaneously.

With a dry hauteur in keeping with the décor and frowning as he stepped forwards, Belloir inquired, 'Monsieur?' – while at the same time Van Damme, in an effort to summon up his usual bonhomie, held out his hand to Maigret and exclaimed, 'What a surprise! Imagine seeing you here!'

The third man silently took in the scene in what looked like complete bafflement.

'Please excuse me for disturbing you,' began the inspector. 'I did not expect to be interrupting a meeting this early in the morning . . .'

'Not at all! Not at all!' replied Van Damme. 'Do sit down! Cigar?'

There was a box on the mahogany desk. He hurried to open it and select a Havana, talking all the while.

'Hold on, I'm looking for my lighter . . . You're not going to write me a ticket because these are missing their tobacco tax stamp, are you? But why didn't you tell me in Bremen that you knew Belloir! When I think that we might have made the trip together! I left a few hours after you did: a telegram, some business requiring my presence in Paris. And I've taken advantage of it to come and say hello to Belloir . . .'

The latter, having lost none of his starchy manner, kept looking from one to the other of the two men as if waiting for an explanation, and it was towards him that Maigret turned and spoke.

'I'll make my visit as short as possible, given that you're expecting someone . . .'

'I am? How do you know?'

'Simple! Your maid told me that I was expected. And as I cannot be the person in question, then clearly . . .'

His eyes were laughing in spite of himself, but his face stayed perfectly blank.

'Inspector Maigret, of the Police Judiciaire. Perhaps you noticed me yesterday evening at the Café de Paris, where I was seeking information relevant to an ongoing investigation.'

'It can't be that incident in Bremen, surely?' remarked Van Damme, with feigned indifference.

'The very one! Would you be so kind, Monsieur Belloir, as to look at this photograph and tell me if this is indeed the man you invited into your home one night last week?'

He held out a picture of the dead man. The deputy bank director looked at it, but vacantly, without seeing it.

'I don't know this person!' he stated, returning the photo to Maigret.

'You're certain this isn't the man who spoke to you when you were returning home from the Café de Paris?'

'What are you talking about?'

'Forgive me if I seem to labour the point, but I need some information that is, after all, of only minor importance, and I took the liberty of disturbing you at home because I assumed you would not mind helping us in our inquiries. On that evening, a drunk was sitting near the third billiard table, where you were playing. All the customers noticed him. He left shortly before you did, and later on, after you'd left your friends, he approached you.'

'I have a vague recollection . . . He asked me for a light.'

'And you came back here with him, isn't that right?'

Belloir smiled rather nastily.

'I've no idea who told you such nonsense. I'm hardly the sort of person to bring home tramps.'

'You might have recognized him – as an old friend, or . . .'

'I have better taste in friends!'

'You're saying that you went home alone?'

'Absolutely.'

'Was that man the same one in the photo I just showed you?'

'I have no idea. I never even looked at him.'

Listening with obvious impatience, Van Damme had been on the verge of interrupting several times. As for the third man, who had a short brown beard and was dressed all in black in a bygone but 'artistic' fashion, he was looking out of the window, occasionally wiping away the fog his breath left on the pane.

'In which case, I must now simply thank you and apologize once again, Monsieur Belloir.'

'Just a minute, inspector!' exclaimed Joseph Van Damme. 'You're not going to leave just like that? Please, do stay here with us for a moment, and Belloir will offer us some of that fine brandy he always keeps on hand . . . Do you realize that I'm rather put out with you for not coming to dinner with me, in Bremen? I waited for you all evening!'

'Did you travel here by train?'

'By plane! I almost always fly, like most businessmen, in fact! Then, in Paris, I felt like dropping in on my old friend Belloir. We were at university together.'

'In Liège?'

'Yes. And it's almost ten years now since we last saw each other. I didn't even know that he'd got married! It's odd to find him again – with a fine young son! But . . . are you really still working on that suicide of yours?'

Belloir had rung for the maid, whom he told to bring brandy and some glasses. His every move was made slowly and carefully, but with each move he betrayed the gnawing uncertainty he felt.

'The investigation has only just begun,' said Maigret quietly. 'It's impossible to tell if it will be a long one or if the case will be all wrapped up in a day or two.'

When the front doorbell rang, the other three men exchanged furtive glances. Voices were heard; then someone with a strong Belgian accent asked, 'Are they all upstairs? Don't bother, I know the way.'

From the doorway he called out, 'Hello, fellows!'

And met with dead silence. When he saw Maigret, he looked questioningly at the others.

'Weren't you . . . expecting me?'

Belloir's expression tightened. Walking over to the inspector, he said, as if through clenched teeth, 'Jef Lombard, a friend.'

Then, pronouncing every syllable distinctly: 'Inspector Maigret, of the Police Judiciaire.'

The new arrival gave a little start, and stammered in a flat voice that squeaked in the most peculiar way, 'Aha! . . . I see . . . Well, fine . . .'

After which, in his bewilderment, he gave his overcoat to the maid, only to chase after her to retrieve the cigarettes he had left in a pocket.

'Another Belgian, inspector,' observed Van Damme. 'Yes, you're witnessing a real Belgian reunion! You must think this all looks like a conspiracy . . . What about that brandy, Belloir? Inspector, a cigar? Jef Lombard is the only one who still lives in Liège. It just so happens that business affairs have brought us all to the same place at the same moment, so we've decided to celebrate, and have a grand old time! And I wonder if . . .'

He hesitated for a moment, looking around at the others.

'You skipped that dinner I wanted to treat you to in Bremen. Why not have lunch with us later today?'

'Unfortunately, I have other engagements,' replied Maigret. 'Besides, I've already taken enough of your time.'

Jef Lombard had gone over to a table. He was pale, with irregular features, so tall and thin that his limbs seemed too long for his body.

'Ah! Here's the picture I was looking for,' muttered Maigret, as if to himself. 'I won't ask you, Monsieur Lombard, if you know this man, because that would be one chance in a million . . .'

But he contrived to show him the photo anyway – and saw the man's Adam's apple seem to swell, bobbing weirdly up and down.

'Don't know him,' Lombard managed to croak.

Belloir's manicured fingers were drumming on his desk, while Van Damme cast about for something to say.

'So, inspector, I won't have the pleasure of seeing you again? You're going straight back to Paris?'

'I'm not sure yet. My apologies, gentlemen.'

Van Damme shook hands with him, so the others had to as well. Belloir's hand was hard and dry. The bearded man's handshake was more hesitant, and Jef Lombard was off in a corner of the study lighting a cigarette, so he simply nodded towards Maigret and grunted.

Maigret brushed past the green plant in its enormous porcelain pot and went back down the stairs with their brass carpet rods. In the front hall, over the shrill scraping of a violin lesson, he heard a woman's voice saying, 'Slow down . . . Keep your elbow level with your chin . . . Gently!'

It was Madame Belloir and her son. He caught sight of them from the street, through the drawing-room curtains.

It was 2 p.m., and Maigret had just finished lunch at the Café de Paris when he noticed Van Damme come in and look around as if searching for someone. Spotting Maigret, he smiled and came over with his hand out-stretched.

'So this is what you call having other engagements! Eating alone in a restaurant! I understand: you wanted to leave us in peace.'

He was clearly one of those people who latch on to you without any invitation, ignoring any suggestion that their attentions might be unwelcome.

Maigret took selfish pleasure in his chilly response, but Van Damme sat down at his table anyway.

'You've finished? In that case, allow me to offer you a *digestif*... Waiter! Well, what will you have, inspector? An old Armagnac?'

He called for the drinks list, and after consultation with the proprietor, chose an 1867 Armagnac, to be served in snifters.

'I was wondering: when are you returning to Paris? I'm going there this afternoon, and since I cannot bear trains, I'll be hiring a car... If you like, I'll take you along. Well, what do you think of my friends?'

He inhaled the aroma of his brandy with a critical air, then pulled a cigar case from his pocket.

'Please, have one, they're quite good. There's only one place in Bremen where you can get them, and they're straight from Havana!'

Maigret had emptied his eyes of all thought and made his face a blank.

'It's funny, meeting again years later,' remarked Van Damme, who seemed unable to cope with silence. 'At the age of twenty, starting out, we're all on the same footing, so to speak. Time passes, and when we get together again, it's astonishing how far away from one another we seem ... I'm not saying anything against them, mind you, it's just that, back at Belloir's house, I felt ... uncomfortable.

That stifling provincial atmosphere! And Belloir himself, quite the clothes horse! Although he hasn't done badly for himself, seeing as he married the daughter of Morvandeau, the one who's in sprung mattresses. All Belloir's brothers-in-law are in industry. And him? He's sitting pretty in the bank, where he'll wind up director one of these days.'

'And the short man with the beard?' asked Maigret.

'That one . . . He may yet find his way and make good. Meanwhile, I think he's feeling the pinch, poor devil. He's a sculptor, in Paris. And talented, it seems – but what do you expect? You saw him, in that get-up from another century . . . Nothing modern about him! And no business sense.'

'Jef Lombard?'

'They don't make them any better! In his younger days, he was a real joker, could keep you laughing yourself silly for hours on end. He was going to be a painter . . . He earned a living as a newspaper artist, then worked as a photoengraver in Liège. He's married. I believe they're expecting their third child.

'What I'm saying is, when I was with them I felt as if I couldn't breathe! Those petty lives, with their petty pre-occupations and worries . . . It isn't their fault, but I can't wait to get back to the business world.'

He drained his glass and considered the almost deserted room, where a waiter at a table in the back was reading a newspaper.

'It's settled, then? You're returning to Paris with me?'

'But aren't you travelling with the short bearded fellow who came with you?'

'Janin? No, by this time he has already taken the train back.'

'Married?'

'Not exactly. But he always has some girlfriend or other who lives with him for a week, a year – and then he gets a new one! Whom he always introduces as "Madame Janin". Oh, waiter! The same again, here!'

Maigret had to be careful, at times, not to let his eyes give away how keenly he was listening. He had left the address of the Café de Paris back at headquarters, and the proprietor now came over to tell him personally that he was wanted on the phone.

News had been wired from Brussels to the Police Judiciaire: *The 30,000-franc notes were handed over by the Banque Générale de Belgique to one Louis Jeunet in payment of a cheque signed by Maurice Belloir.*

Opening the door to leave the telephone booth, Maigret saw that Van Damme, unaware that he was being observed, had allowed himself to drop his mask – and now seemed deflated and, above all, less glowing with health and optimism.

He must have felt those watchful eyes on him, however, for he shuddered, automatically becoming the jovial businessman once again.

'We're set, then?' he called out. 'You're coming with me? *Patron!* Would you arrange for us to be picked up here by car and driven to Paris? A comfortable car! See to it, will you? And in the meantime, let's have another.'

He chewed on the end of his cigar and just for an instant, as he stared down at the marble table, his eyes lost their lustre, while the corners of his mouth drooped as if the tobacco had left a bitter taste in his mouth.

'It's when you live abroad that you really appreciate the wines and liqueurs of France!'

His words rang hollow, echoing in the abyss lying between them and the man's troubled mind.

Jef Lombard went by in the street, his silhouette slightly blurred by the tulle curtains. He was alone. He walked with long strides, slowly and sadly, seeing nothing of the city all around him.

He was carrying an overnight bag, and Maigret found himself thinking about those two yellow suitcases . . . Lombard's was of better quality, though, with two straps and a sleeve for a calling card. The man's shoe heels were starting to wear down on one side, and his clothes did not look as if anyone brushed them regularly. Jef Lombard was walking all the way to the station.

Van Damme, sporting a large platinum signet ring on one finger, was wreathing himself in a fragrant cloud of cigar smoke heightened by the alcohol's sharp bouquet. Off in the background, the proprietor could be heard on the phone, arranging for the car.

Belloir was probably setting out from his new house for the marble portal of the bank, while his wife took their son for a walk along the avenues. Everyone would wish Belloir a good afternoon. His father-in-law was the biggest businessman around. His brothers-in-law were 'in industry'. A bright future lay ahead of him.

As for Janin, with his black goatee and his artistic *lavallière* bow tie, he was on his way to Paris – in third class, Maigret would have bet on it.

And down at the bottom of the heap was the pale traveller of Neuschanz and Bremen, the husband of the herbalist in Rue Picpus, the milling machine operator from Rue de la Roquette, the solitary drinker who went to gaze at his wife through the shop window, sent himself banknotes as if they were a package of old newspapers, bought sausages in rolls at a station buffet and shot himself in the mouth because he'd been robbed of an old suit that wasn't even his.

'Ready, inspector?'

Maigret flinched and stared in confusion at Van Damme, his gaze so vacant that the other man tried uneasily to laugh and botched it, stammering, 'Were you daydreaming? Wherever you were, it was far away . . . I suspect it's that suicide of yours you're still worried about.'

Not entirely. When startled from his reverie, Maigret – and even he did not know why – had been concentrating on an unusual list, counting up the children involved in this case: one in Rue Picpus, a small figure between his mother and grandmother in a shop smelling of mint and rubber; one in Rheims, who was learning to hold his elbow up by his chin while drawing his bow across the strings of a violin; two in Liège, in the home of Jef Lombard, where a third was on the way . . .

'One last Armagnac, what do you say?'

'Thank you: I've had enough.'

'Come on! We'll have a stirrup cup, or in our case one for the road!'

Only Joseph Van Damme laughed, as he constantly felt he must, like a little boy so afraid to go down into the cellar that he tries to whistle up some courage.

5. Breakdown at Luzancy

As they drove at a fast clip through the gathering dusk, there was hardly a moment's silence. Joseph Van Damme was never at a loss for words and, fuelled by the Armagnac, he managed to keep up a stream of convivial patter. The vehicle was an old sedan, a saloon car with worn cushions, flower holders and marquetry side pockets. The driver was wearing a trench coat, with a knitted scarf around his neck.

They had been driving for about two hours when the driver pulled over to the side of the road and stopped at least a kilometre from a village, a few lights of which gleamed in the misty evening.

After inspecting the rear wheels, the driver informed his passengers that he had found a flat tyre, which it would take him fifteen minutes or so to repair.

The two men got out. The driver was already settling a jack under the rear axle and assured them that he did not need any help.

Was it Maigret or Van Damme who suggested a short walk? Neither of them, actually; it seemed only natural for them to walk a little way along the road, where they noticed a path leading down to the rushing waters of a river.

'Look! The Marne!' said Van Damme. 'It's in spate . . .'

As they strolled slowly along the little path, smoking

their cigars, they heard a noise that puzzled them until they reached the riverbank.

A hundred metres away, across the water, they saw the lock at Luzancy: its gates were closed, and there was no one around. Right at their feet was a dam, with its milky overspill, churning waters and powerful current. The Marne was running high.

In the darkness they could just make out branches, perhaps entire trees, smashing repeatedly into the barrier until swept at last over its edge.

The only light came from the lock, on the far side of the river.

Joseph Van Damme kept talking away.

'Every year the Germans make tremendous efforts to harness the energy of rivers, and the Russians are right behind them: in the Ukraine they're constructing a dam that'll cost 120 million dollars but will provide electricity to three provinces.'

It was almost unnoticeable, the way his voice faltered – briefly – at the word *electricity*. And then, coughing, Van Damme had to take out his handkerchief to blow his nose.

They were on the very brink of the river. Shoved suddenly from behind, Maigret lost his balance, turning as he fell forwards, and grabbed the edge of the grassy riverbank with both hands, his feet now in the water, while his hat was already plunging over the dam.

The rest happened quickly, for he had been expecting that push. Clods of earth were giving way under his right hand, but he had spotted a branch sturdy enough for him to cling to with his other hand.

Only seconds later, he was on his knees on the towpath and then on his feet, shouting at a figure fading away.

'Stop!'

It was strange: Van Damme didn't dare run. He was heading towards the car in only a modest hurry and kept looking back, his legs wobbly with shock.

And he allowed himself to be overtaken. With his head down and pulled like a turtle's into the collar of his overcoat, he simply swung his fist once through the air, in rage, as if he were pounding on an imaginary table and growled through clenched teeth, 'Idiot!'

Just to be safe, Maigret had brought out his revolver. Gun in hand, without taking his eyes off the other man, he shook the legs of his trousers, soaked to the knees, while water spurted from his shoes.

Back at the road, the driver was tapping on the horn to let them know that the car was roadworthy again.

'Let's go!' said the inspector.

And they took their same seats in the car, in silence. Van Damme still had his cigar between his teeth but he would not meet Maigret's eyes.

Ten kilometres. Twenty kilometres. They slowed down to go through a town, where people were going about their business in the lighted streets. Then it was back to the highway.

'You still can't arrest me, though,' said Van Damme abruptly, and Maigret started with surprise. And yet these words – so unexpected, spoken so slowly, even stubbornly – had echoed his own misgivings . . .

They reached Meaux. Countryside gave way to the outer suburbs. A light rain began to fall, and whenever the car passed a streetlamp, each drop became a star. Then the inspector leaned forwards to speak into the voice-pipe.

'You're to take us to the Police Judiciaire, Quai des Orfèvres.'

He filled a pipe he could not smoke because his matches were now wet. Van Damme's face was almost completely turned away from him and further obscured in the dim light, but he could sense the man's fury.

There was now a hard edge to the atmosphere, something rancorous and intense.

Maigret himself had his chin thrust out belligerently.

This tension led to a ridiculous incident after the car pulled up in front of the Préfecture and the men got out, the inspector first.

'Come along!'

The driver was waiting to be paid, but Van Damme was ignoring him. There was a moment of hesitation, indecision.

'Well?' said Maigret, not unaware of the absurdity of the situation. 'You're the one who hired the car.'

'Pardon me: if I travelled as your prisoner, it's up to you to pay.'

A small matter, but didn't it show how much had happened since Rheims and, most importantly, how much the Belgian businessman had changed?

Maigret paid and silently showed Van Damme to his office. After closing the door behind him, the first thing he did was to stir up the fire in the stove.

Next he took some clothing from a cupboard and, without a glance at the other man, changed his trousers, shoes and socks and placed his damp things near the stove to dry.

Van Damme had sat down without waiting to be asked. In the bright light, the change in him was even more striking: he'd left his bogus bonhomie, his open manner and somewhat strained smile back at Luzancy and now, with a grim and cunning look, he was waiting.

Pretending to pay him no attention, Maigret kept busy for a little while around his office, organizing dossiers, telephoning his boss for some information that had nothing to do with the current case.

Finally, he went over to confront Van Damme.

'When, where and how did you first meet the man who committed suicide in Bremen and who was travelling with a passport in the name of Louis Jeunet?'

The other man flinched almost imperceptibly but faced his challenger with bold composure.

'Why am I here?'

'You refuse to answer my question?'

Van Damme laughed, but now his laughter was cold and sarcastic.

'I know the law as well as you do, inspector. Either you charge me and must show me the arrest warrant, or you don't charge me and I don't have to answer you. And in the first case, the law allows me to wait for the assistance of a lawyer before speaking to you.'

Maigret did not seem angry or even annoyed by the man's attitude. On the contrary! He studied him with curiosity and perhaps a certain satisfaction.

Thanks to the incident at Luzancy, Joseph Van Damme had been forced to abandon his play-acting and the pretence he had kept up not only with Maigret, but with everyone else and even, in the end, with himself.

There was almost nothing left of the jolly, shallow businessman from Bremen, constantly on the go between his modern office and the finest taverns and restaurants. Gone was the happy-go-lucky operator raking in money with zestful energy and a taste for the good life. All that remained was a haggard face drained of colour, and it was uncanny how quickly dark, puffy circles seemed to have appeared under his eyes.

Only an hour earlier, hadn't Van Damme still been a free man who, although he did have something on his conscience, yet enjoyed the self-assurance guaranteed by his broker's licence, his reputation, his money and his shrewdness?

And he himself had emphasized this change.

In Rheims, he was used to standing round after round of drinks. He offered his guests the finest cigars. He had only to give an order, and a café proprietor would hasten to curry favour, phoning a garage to hire their most comfortable car.

He was somebody!

In Paris? He had refused to pay for the trip. He invoked the law. He appeared ready to argue, to defend himself at every turn, fiercely, like a man fighting for his life.

And he was furious with himself! His angry exclamation after what had happened on the bank of the Marne was proof of that. There had been no premeditation. He hadn't known the driver. Even when they had stopped for the flat tyre, he hadn't immediately realized how that might work to his advantage.

Only when they had reached the water . . . The swirling current, the trees swept by as if they were simply dead leaves . . . Like a fool, without thinking twice, he'd given that push with his shoulder.

Now he was beside himself. He was sure that the inspector had been waiting for that move! He probably even realized that he was done for – and was all the more determined to strike back with everything he had.

When he went to light a new cigar, Maigret snatched it from his mouth, tossed it into the coal scuttle – and for good measure removed the hat Van Damme hadn't bothered to take off.

'For your information,' said the Belgian, 'I have business to attend to. If you do not mean to officially arrest me in accordance with the regulations, I must ask you to be good enough to release me. If you don't, I'll be forced to file a complaint for false imprisonment.

'With regard to your little dip in the river, I might as well tell you that I'll deny everything: the towpath was soggy and you slipped in the mud. The driver will confirm that I never tried to run away, as I would have if I'd really tried to drown you.

'As for the rest, I still don't know what you might have against me. I came to Paris on business and I can prove that. Then I went to Rheims to see an old friend, an upstanding citizen like myself.

'After meeting you in Bremen, where we don't often see Frenchmen, I was trusting enough to consider you a friend, taking you out for dinner and drinks and then offering you a ride back to Paris.

'You showed me and my friends the photograph of a man we do not know. A man who killed himself! That's been materially proved. No one has lodged a complaint, so you have no grounds for taking action.

'And that's all I have to say to you.'

Maigret stuck a twist of paper into the stove, lit his pipe

and remarked, almost as an afterthought, 'You're perfectly free to go.'

He could not help smiling to see Van Damme so dumbfounded by his suspiciously easy victory.

'What do you mean?'

'That you're free, that's all! May I add that I'm quite ready to return your hospitality and invite you to dinner.'

Rarely had he felt so light-hearted. The other man gaped at him in amazement, almost in fear, as if the inspector's words had been heavy with hidden threats. Warily, Van Damme rose to his feet.

'I'm free to return to Bremen?'

'Why not? You just said yourself that you've committed no crime.'

For an instant, it seemed that Van Damme might recover his confidence and bluster, might even accept that dinner invitation and explain away the incident at Luzancy as clumsiness or a momentary aberration . . .

But the smile on Maigret's face snuffed out that flicker of optimism. Van Damme grabbed his hat and clapped it on to his head.

'How much do I owe you for the car?'

'Nothing at all. Only too happy to have been of service.'

Van Damme was at such a loss for words that his lips were trembling, and he had no idea how to leave gracefully. In the end he shrugged and walked out, muttering, 'Idiot!'

But it was impossible to tell what or whom he meant by that.

Out on the staircase, as Maigret leaned over the handrail to watch him go, he was still saying it over and over . . .

Sergeant Lucas happened along with some files, on his way to his boss's office.

'Quick! Get your hat and coat: follow that man to the ends of the earth if you have to . . .'

And Maigret plucked the files from his subordinate's hands.

The inspector had just finished filling out various requests for information, each headed by a different name. Sent out to the appropriate divisions, these forms would return to him with detailed reports on these persons of interest: Maurice Belloir, a native of Liège, deputy director of a bank, Rue de Vesle, Rheims; Jef Lombard, photoengraver in Liège; Gaston Janin, sculptor, Rue Lepic, Paris; and Joseph Van Damme, import-export commission agent in Bremen.

He was filling out the last form when the office boy announced that a man wanted to see him regarding the suicide of Louis Jeunet.

It was late. Headquarters was practically deserted, although an inspector was typing a report in the neighbouring office.

'Come!'

Ushered in, his visitor stopped at the door, looking awkward and ill at ease, as if he might already be sorry to have come.

'Sit down, why don't you!'

Maigret had taken his measure: tall, thin, with whitish-blond hair, poorly shaved, wearing shabby clothes rather like Louis Jeunet's. His overcoat was missing a button, the collar was soiled, and the lapels in need of a brushing.

From a few other tiny signs – a certain attitude, a way

of sitting down and looking around – the inspector recognized an ex-con, someone whose papers may all be in order but who still cannot help being nervous around the police.

'You're here because of the photo? Why didn't you come in right away? That picture appeared in the papers two days ago.'

'I don't read them,' the man explained. 'But my wife happened to bring some shopping home wrapped in a bit of newspaper.'

Maigret realized that he'd seen this somewhere before, this constantly shifting expression, this nervous twitching and most of all, the morbid anxiety in the man's eyes.

'Did you know Louis Jeunet?'

'I'm not sure. It isn't a good photo. But I think . . . I believe he's my brother.'

Maigret couldn't help it: he sighed with relief. He felt that this time the whole mystery would be cleared up at last. And he went to stand with his back to the stove, as he often did when in a good mood.

'In which case, your name would be Jeunet?'

'No, but that's it, that's why I hesitated to come here, and yet – he really is my brother! I'm sure of that, now that I see a better photo on the desk . . . That scar, for example! But I don't understand why he killed himself – or why in the world he would change his name.'

'And yours is . . .'

'Armand Lecocq d'Arneville. I brought my papers.'

And there again, that way he reached into his pocket for a grimy passport betrayed his status on the margins of society, someone used to attracting suspicion and proving his identity.

'D'Arneville with a small *d* and an apostrophe?'

'Yes.'

'You were born in Liège,' continued the inspector, consulting the passport. 'You're thirty-five years old. Your profession?'

'At present, I'm an office messenger in a factory at Issy-les-Moulineaux. We live in Grenelle, my wife and I.'

'It says here you're a mechanic.'

'I was one. I've done this and that . . .'

'Even some prison time!' exclaimed Maigret, leafing through the passport. 'You're a deserter.'

'There was an amnesty! Just let me explain . . . My father had money, he ran a tyre business, but I was only six when he abandoned my mother, who'd just given birth to my brother Jean. That's where it all started!

'We moved to a little place in Rue de la Province, in Liège, and in the beginning my father sent us money to live on fairly regularly. He liked to live it up, had mistresses; once, when he came by to drop off our monthly envelope, there was a woman in the car waiting for him down in the street. There were scenes, arguments, and my father stopped paying, or maybe he began paying less and less. My mother worked as a cleaning woman and she gradually went half-mad, not crazy enough to be shut away, but she'd go up to people and pour out her troubles, and she used to roam the streets in tears . . .

'I hardly ever saw my brother. I was off running with the local kids. They must have hauled us in to the police station ten times. Then I was sent to work in a hardware store. My mother was always crying, so I stayed away from home as much as I could. She liked all the old neighbour women to come over so she could wail her heart out with them.

'I joined the army when I was sixteen and asked to be sent to the Congo, but I only lasted a month. For about a week I hid in Matadi, then I stowed away on a passenger steamer bound for Europe. I got caught, served some time, escaped and made it to France, where I worked at all sorts of jobs. I've gone starving hungry, slept in the market here at Les Halles.

'I haven't always been on the up and up, but I swear to you, I've buckled down and been clean for four years. I'm even married now! To a factory worker. She's had to keep her job because I don't earn much and sometimes there's nothing for me . . .

'I've never tried to go back to Belgium. Someone told me that my mother died in a lunatic asylum but that my father's still alive. He never wanted to bother with us, though. He has a second family.'

And the man gave a crooked smile, as if to apologize.

'What about your brother?'

'It was different with him: Jean was serious. He won a scholarship as a boy and went on to secondary school. When I left Belgium for the Congo he was only thirteen, and I haven't seen him since. I heard news now and again, whenever I ran into anyone from Liège. Some people took an interest in him, and he went on to study at the university there. That was ten years ago . . . After that, any Belgians I saw told me they didn't know anything about him, that he must have gone abroad, because he'd dropped out of sight.

'It was a real shock to see the photograph, and especially to think that he'd died in Bremen, under a false name. You can't have any idea . . . Me, I got off to a bad start, I messed up, did stupid things, but when I remember Jean, at thirteen . . . He was like me, but steadier, more serious, already reading poetry. He used to study all by himself at night, reading by the light of candle ends he got from a sacristan. I was sure he'd make it. Listen, even when he was little, he would never have been a street kid, not at any price – and the neighbourhood bad boys even made fun of him!

'But me, I was always short of money, and I wasn't ashamed to hound my mother for it. She used to go without to give me some . . . She adored us. At sixteen, you don't understand! But now I can remember a time when I was mean to her simply because I'd promised some girl I'd take her to the movies . . . Well, my mother had no money. I cried, I threatened her! A charity had just got some medicines for her – and she went and sold them.

'Can you understand? And now it's Jean who's dead, like that, up there, with someone else's name! I don't know what he did. I cannot believe he went down the same wrong road I did. You wouldn't believe it either if you'd known him as a child . . .

'Please, can you tell me anything?'

But Maigret handed the man's passport back to him and asked, 'In Liège, do you know any Belloirs, Van Dammes, Janins, Lombards?'

'A Belloir, yes: the father was a doctor, in our neighbour-hood. The son was a student. But they were well-to-do, respectable people, out of my league.'

'And the others?'

'I've heard the name Van Damme before. I think there was a big grocery store in Rue de la Cathédrale by that name. Oh, it's so long ago now . . .' He seemed to hesitate.

And then Armand Lecocq d'Arneville asked, 'Could I see Jean's body? Has it been brought here?'

'It will arrive in Paris tomorrow.'

'Are you sure that he really did kill himself?'

Maigret looked away, disturbed by the thought that he was more than sure of it: he had witnessed the tragedy and been the unwitting cause of it.

The other man was twisting his cap in his hands, shifting from one foot to the other, awaiting his dismissal. Lost within pale lids, his deep-set eyes with their pupils flecked grey like confetti reminded Maigret so poignantly of the humble, anxious eyes of the traveller from Neuschanz that within his breast the inspector felt a sharp pang that was very like remorse.

6. The Hanged Men

It was nine o'clock in the evening. Maigret was at home in Boulevard Richard-Lenoir in his shirt-sleeves, his collar off, and his wife was sewing when Lucas came in soaked from the downpour outside, shrugging the rain from his shoulders.

'The man left town,' he said. 'Seeing as I wasn't sure if I was supposed to follow him abroad . . .'

'Liège?'

'That's it! You already knew? His luggage was at the Hôtel du Louvre. He had dinner there, changed and took the 6.19 Liège express. Single ticket, first class. He bought a whole slew of magazines at the station newsstand.'

'You'd think he was trying to get underfoot on purpose!' groused the inspector. 'In Bremen, when I've no idea he even exists, he's the one who shows up at the morgue, invites me to lunch and plain latches on to me. I get back to Paris: he's here a few hours before or after I arrive . . . Probably before, because he took a plane. I go to Rheims; he's already there. An hour ago, I decided to return to Liège tomorrow – and he'll be there by this evening! And the last straw? He's well aware that I'm coming and that his presence there almost amounts to an accusation against him.'

Lucas, who knew nothing about the case, ventured a suggestion.

'Maybe he wants to draw suspicion on himself to protect somebody else?'

'Are you talking about a crime?' asked Mme Maigret peaceably, without looking up from her sewing.

But her husband rose with a sigh and looked back at the armchair in which he'd been so comfortable just a moment before.

'How late do the trains run to Belgium?'

'Only the night train is left, at 9.30. It arrives in Liège at around 6 a.m.'

'Would you pack my bag?' Maigret asked his wife. 'Lucas, a little something? Help yourself, you know where everything is in the cabinet. My sister-in-law has just sent us some plum brandy, and she makes it herself, in Alsace. It's the bottle with the long neck . . .'

He dressed, removed clothing B from the yellow suitcase and placed it, well wrapped, in his travel bag. Half an hour later, he left with Lucas, and they waited outside for a taxi.

'What case is this?' Lucas asked. 'I haven't heard anything about it around the shop.'

'I hardly know myself!' the inspector exclaimed. 'A very strange fellow died, in a way that makes no sense, right in front of me – and *that* incident is all tied up in the most ungodly tangle of events, which I'm attempting to figure out. I'm charging blindly at it like a wild boar and wouldn't be surprised if I wound up getting my knuckles rapped . . . Here's a taxi. Shall I drop you off somewhere?'

It was eight in the morning when Maigret left the Hôtel du Chemin de Fer, across from Gare des Guillemins, in

Liège. He'd taken a bath, shaved and was carrying a package containing not all of clothing B, just the suit jacket.

He found Rue Haute-Sauvenière, a steep and busy street, where he asked for directions to Morcel's. In the dim light of the tailor's shop, a man in shirt-sleeves examined the jacket, turning it over and over carefully while questioning the inspector.

'It's old,' he finally announced, 'and it's torn. That's about all I can tell you.'

'Nothing else comes to mind?'

'Not a thing. The collar's poorly cut. It's imitation English woollen cloth, made in Verviers.'

And then the man became more chatty.

'You're French? Does this jacket belong to someone you know?'

With a sigh, Maigret retrieved the suit jacket as the man nattered on and at last wound up where he ought to have started.

'You see, I've only been here for the past six months. If I'd made the suit in question, it wouldn't have had time to wear out like that.'

'And Monsieur Morcel?'

'In Robermont!'

'Is that far from here?'

The tailor laughed, tickled by the misunderstanding.

'Robermont, that's our cemetery. Monsieur Morcel died at the beginning of this year, and I took over his business.'

Back out in the street with his package under his arm, Maigret headed for Rue Hors-Château, one of the oldest streets in the city, where, at the far end of a courtyard, he found a zinc plaque announcing: *Photogravure Centrale – Jef Lombard – Rapid results for work of all kinds.*

The windows had small panes, in the style of historic Liège, and in the centre of the courtyard of small, uneven paving stones was a fountain bearing the sculpted coat of arms of some great lord of long ago.

The inspector rang. He heard footsteps coming down from the first floor, and an old woman peeked out from the ancient-looking door.

'Just push it open,' she said, pointing to a glazed door. 'The workshop's all the way at the end of the passage.'

A long room, lit by a glass roof; two men in blue overalls working among zinc plates and tubs full of acids; a floor strewn with photographic proofs and paper smeared with thick, greasy ink.

The walls were crowded with posters, advertisements, magazine covers.

'Monsieur Lombard?'

'He's in the office, with a gentleman. Please come this way – and don't get any ink on you! Take a left turn, then it's the first door.'

The building must have been constructed piecemeal; stairs went up and down, and doors opened on to abandoned rooms.

The feeling was both antiquated and weirdly cheerful, like the old woman who'd greeted him downstairs and the atmosphere in the workroom.

Coming to a shadowy corridor, the inspector heard voices and thought he recognized that of Joseph Van Damme. He tried in vain to make out the words, and when he took a few steps closer, the voices stopped. A man stuck his head out of the half-open door: it was Jef Lombard.

'Is it for me?' he called, not recognizing his visitor in the half-light.

The office was smaller than the other rooms and furnished with two chairs, shelves full of photographic negatives and a table cluttered with bills, prospectuses and business letters from various companies.

And perched on a corner of the table was Van Damme, who nodded vaguely in Maigret's direction and then sat perfectly still, scowling and staring straight ahead.

Jef Lombard was in his work clothes; his hands were dirty, and there were tiny blackish flecks on his face.

'May I help you?'

He cleared papers off a chair, which he pushed over to his visitor, and then he looked around for the cigarette butt he'd left balanced on the edge of a wooden shelf now beginning to char.

'Just some information,' replied the inspector, without sitting down. 'I'm sorry to bother you, but I'd like to know if, a few years ago, you ever knew a certain Jean Lecocq d'Arneville . . .'

There was a quick, distinct change. Van Damme shuddered, but resisted turning towards Maigret, while Lombard bent abruptly down to pick up a crumpled paper lying on the floor.

'I . . . may have heard that name before,' murmured the photoengraver. 'He . . . From Liège, isn't he?'

The colour had drained from his face. He moved a pile of plates from one spot to another.

'I don't know what became of him. I . . . It was so long ago . . .'

'Jef! Jef, hurry!'

It was a woman's voice, coming from the labyrinth of

stairs and corridors, and she arrived at the open door breathless from running, so excited that her legs were shaky and she had to wipe her face with a corner of her apron. Maigret recognized the old lady he'd seen downstairs.

'Jef!'

And he, now even whiter from emotion, his eyes gleaming, gasped, 'Well?'

'A girl! Hurry!'

The man looked around, stammered something impossible to decipher and dashed out of the door.

Alone with Maigret, Van Damme pulled a cigar from his pocket, lit it slowly, crushed out the match with his shoe. He wore the same wooden expression as in Maigret's office: his mouth was set in the same hard line, and he ground his jaws in the same way.

But the inspector pretended not to notice him and, hands in his pockets, pipe between his teeth, he began to walk around the office, examining the walls.

Very little of the original wallpaper was still visible, however, because any space not taken up by shelves was covered with drawings, etchings, and paintings that were simply canvases on stretchers without frames, rather plodding landscapes in which the tree foliage and grass were of the same even, pasty green.

There were a few caricatures signed *Jef*, some of them touched up with watercolours, some cut from a local paper.

What struck Maigret, though, was how many of the drawings were all variations on one particular theme. The drawing paper had yellowed with age, and a few dates indicated that these sketches had been done about ten years earlier.

They were executed in a different style as well, with a more darkly Romantic sensibility, and seemed like the efforts of a young art student imitating the work of Gustave Doré.

A first ink drawing showed a hanged man swinging from a gallows on which perched an enormous crow. And there were at least twenty other etchings and pen or pencil sketches that had the same leitmotif of hanging.

On the edge of a forest: a man hanging from every branch.

A church steeple: beneath the weathercock, a human body dangling from each arm of the cross.

There were hanged men of all kinds. Some were dressed in the fashions of the sixteenth century and formed a kind of Court of Miracles, where everybody was swinging a few feet above the ground.

There was one crazy hanged man in a top hat and tails, cane in hand, whose gallows was a lamp post.

Below another sketch were written four lines from François Villon's *Ballad of the Hanged Men*.

There were dates, always from around the same time, and all these macabre pictures from ten years earlier were now displayed along with captioned sketches for comic papers, drawings for calendars and almanacs, landscapes of the surrounding Ardennes and advertising posters.

Another recurrent theme was the steeple – in fact, so was the whole church, depicted from the front, from the sides, from below. The church portal, on its own. The gargoyles. The parvis, with its six steps looming large in perspective . . .

Always the same church! And as Maigret moved from one wall to another, he could sense Van Damme's growing agitation, an uneasiness fuelled, perhaps, by the same temptation that had overwhelmed him by the dam at Luzancy.

A quarter of an hour passed like this, and then Jef Lombard returned, his eyes moist with emotion, wiping his hand across his forehead and brushing away a stray lock of hair.

'Please forgive me,' he said. 'My wife has just given birth. A girl!'

There was a hint of pride in his voice, but, as he spoke, he was looking anxiously back and forth between Maigret and Van Damme.

'Our third child. But I'm still as excited as I was the first time! You saw my mother-in-law, well – she had eleven and she's sobbing with joy, she's gone to give the workmen the good news and wants them to see our baby girl.'

His eyes followed Maigret's gaze, now fixed upon the two men hanging from the church-steeple cross, and he became even more nervous.

'The sins of my youth,' he murmured, clearly uncomfortable. 'Terrible stuff. But at the time I thought I was going to be a great artist . . .'

'It's a church in Liège?'

Jef didn't answer right away. And when he finally did, it was almost with regret.

'It's been gone for seven years. They tore it down to build a new church. The old one wasn't beautiful, it didn't even have any style to speak of, but it was very old, with a touch of mystery in all its lines and in the little streets and alleys around it . . . They've all been levelled now.'

'What was its name?'

'The Church of Saint-Pholien. The new one is in the same place and bears the same name.'

Still seated on the corner of Lombard's table, Joseph Van Damme was fidgeting as if his nerves were burning him inside, an inner turmoil betrayed only by the faintest of movements, uneven breathing, a trembling in his fingers, and the way one foot was jiggling against a table leg.

'Were you married at that time?' continued Maigret.

Lombard laughed.

'I was nineteen! I was studying at the Académie des Beaux-Arts. Look over there . . .'

And he pointed, with a look of fond nostalgia, to a clumsy portrait in gloomy colours that was nevertheless recognizable as him, thanks to the telling irregularity of his features. His hair was almost shoulder length; he wore a black tunic buttoned up to his neck and an ample *lavallière* bow tie.

The painting was flagrantly Romantic, even to the traditional death's-head in the background.

'If you'd told me back then that I'd wind up a photo-engraver!' he marvelled, with helpless irony.

Jef Lombard seemed equally unsettled by Van Damme and Maigret, but he clearly had no idea how to get them to leave.

A workman came for advice about a plate that wasn't ready.

'Have them come back this afternoon.'

'But they say that will be too late!'

'So what! Tell them I've just had a daughter . . .'

Lombard's eyes, his movements, the pallor of his complexion pocked with tiny acid marks – everything about him reflected a disturbing confusion of joy, anxiety, perhaps even anguish.

'If I may, I'd like to offer you something . . . We'll go down to the house.'

The three men walked back along the maze of corridors and through the door where the old woman had spoken to Maigret. There were blue tiles in the hall and a clean smell faintly scented, however, with a kind of staleness, perhaps from the stuffiness of the lying-in room.

'The two boys are at my brother-in-law's. Come through here . . .'

He opened the door to the dining room, where the small panes of the windows admitted a dim, bleak light that glinted off the many copper pieces on display everywhere. The furniture was dark.

On the wall was a large portrait of a woman, signed *Jef*, full of awkward passages but imbued with a clear desire to present the model – presumably the artist's wife – in a flattering way.

When Maigret looked around the room he was not surprised to find more hanged men. The best ones, considered good enough to frame!

'You'll have a glass of genever?'

The inspector could feel Van Damme glaring coldly at him, obviously infuriated by the whole situation.

'You were saying a moment ago that you knew Jean Lecocq d'Arneville . . .'

Steps sounded on the floor above, probably from the lying-in room.

'But only casually,' the distracted father replied, listening intently to the faint whimpering of the newborn infant.

And raising his glass, he exclaimed, 'To the health of my little girl! And my wife!'

Turning abruptly away, he drained his glass in one go, then went to the sideboard and pretended to look for something while he recovered from his emotions, but Maigret still caught the soft hiccup of a stifled sob.

'I'm sorry, I have to go up there! On a day like today . . .'

Maigret and Van Damme had not exchanged one word. As they crossed the courtyard, passing by the fountain, the inspector glanced with a faint smile at the other man, wondering what he would do next.

Once out in the street, however, Van Damme simply touched the brim of his hat and strode off to the right.

There aren't many taxis in Liège. Unfamiliar with the tram lines, Maigret walked back to the Hôtel du Chemin de Fer, where he had lunch and made inquiries about the local newspapers.

At two o'clock, he entered the *La Meuse* newspaper building at the very moment when Joseph Van Damme was leaving it: the two men passed silently within arm's reach of each other.

'He's still one step ahead of me!' Maigret grumbled under his breath.

When he asked the usher with his silver chain of office about consulting the newspaper's archives, he was told to fill out an authorization form and wait for its approval.

Maigret thought over certain striking details in his case: Armand Lecocq d'Arneville had told him that his brother had left Liège at around the same time that Jef Lombard was drawing hanged men with such morbid fascination.

And clothing B, which the tramp of Neuschanz and Bremen had carried around in the yellow suitcase, was at least six years old, according to the German technician, *and perhaps even ten . . .*

And now Joseph Van Damme had turned up at *La Meuse*! Didn't that tell the inspector something?

The usher showed Maigret into a room with heavy formal furniture, where the parquet gleamed like a skating rink.

'Which year's collection do you wish to consult?'

Maigret had already noticed the enormous cardboard cases arrayed around the entire room, each containing the issues of a particular year.

'I'll find it myself, thank you.'

The room smelled of polish, musty paper and formal luxury. On the moleskin tabletop were reading stands to hold the cumbersome volumes. Everything was so neat, so clean, so austere that the inspector hardly dared take his pipe from his pocket.

In a few moments he was leafing page by page through the newspapers of the 'year of the hanged men'.

Thousands of headlines streamed past his gaze, some recalling events of worldwide importance, others dealing with local incidents: a big department store fire (a full page for three days running), an alderman's resignation, an increase in tram fares.

Suddenly: torn newsprint, all along the binding. The daily paper for 15 February had been ripped out.

Hurrying into the reception room, Maigret fetched the usher.

'Someone came here before I did, isn't that right? And it was this same collection he asked for?'

'Yes. He was here only five minutes or so.'

'Are you from Liège? Do you remember what happened back then?'

'Ten years ago? Hmm . . . That's the year my sister-in-law died . . . I know! The big floods! We even had to wait a week for the burial because the only way you could get around in the streets down by the Meuse was by boat. Here, look at these articles: *The King and Queen visit the disaster victims* . . . There are photos, and – wait, we're missing an issue. How extraordinary! I'll have to inform the director about this . . .'

Maigret picked up a scrap of newsprint that had fallen to the floor while Joseph Van Damme – and there was no doubt about it – had been tearing out the pages for 15 February.

7. The Three Men

There are four daily papers in Liège. Maigret spent two hours checking their archives one after the other and, as he expected, they were all missing the 15 February issue.

With its luxury department stores, popular brasseries, cinemas and dance halls, the place to see and be seen in Liège is the busy quadrangle of streets known as the Carré. At least three times, the inspector caught sight of Joseph Van Damme strolling around there, walking stick in hand.

When Maigret returned to the Hôtel du Chemin de Fer, he found two messages waiting for him. The first was a telegram from Lucas, to whom he had given certain instructions just before leaving Paris.

> Stove ashes found room Louis Jeunet Rue Roquette analysed by technician stop Identified remains Belgian and French banknotes stop Quantity suggests large sum

The other was a letter delivered to the hotel by messenger, typed on ordinary typing paper without any heading.

> Detective Chief Inspector,
>
> I beg to inform you that I am prepared to furnish the answers you seek in your inquiry.
>
> I have my reasons for being cautious, and I would be obliged, if my proposal interests you, if you would meet me this evening at around eleven o'clock, at the Café de

la Bourse, which is behind the Théâtre Royal.

Until then, I remain, sir, your most humble, loyal and obedient servant, etc., etc.

No signature. On the other hand, a rather surprising number of business turns of phrase for a note of this kind: *I beg to inform you . . . I would be obliged . . . if my proposal interests you . . . your most humble, loyal and obedient servant, etc., etc. . . .*

Dining alone at his table, Maigret realized that, although he hadn't much noticed it before, the focus of his attention had shifted somewhat away from Jean Lecocq d'Arneville, who had killed himself in a hotel room in Bremen under the name of Louis Jeunet.

Now the inspector found himself haunted by the images Jef Lombard had hung up everywhere, those hanged men dangling from a church-steeple cross, from the trees in a wood, from a nail in an attic room, grotesque or sinister hanged men in the garb of many centuries, their faces livid or flushed crimson.

At half past ten he set out for the Théâtre Royal; it was five to eleven when he pushed open the door of the Café de la Bourse, a quiet little place frequented by locals and by card players in particular.

And there he found a surprise waiting for him. Three men were sitting at a table off in a corner, over by the counter: Maurice Belloir, Jef Lombard and Joseph Van Damme.

Things seemed to hang fire for a moment while the waiter helped Maigret out of his overcoat. Belloir automatically rose halfway in greeting. Van Damme didn't move a muscle. Lombard, grimacing with extraordinary nervous tension, could not keep still as he waited for his companions to make a move.

Was Maigret going to come over, shake hands, sit down with them? He knew them all: he had accepted Van Damme's invitation to lunch in Bremen, he'd had a glass of brandy at Belloir's house in Rheims, and only that morning he had visited Lombard's home.

'Good evening, gentlemen.'

He shook their hands with his customary firmness, which could at times seem vaguely threatening.

'Imagine, meeting you all again like this!'

There was space next to Van Damme on the banquette, so Maigret parked himself there.

'A glass of pale ale!' he called to the waiter.

Then silence fell. A strained, oppressive silence. Van Damme stared straight ahead, his teeth clenched. Lombard was still fidgeting, as if his clothes were too tight at his armpits. Belloir, cold and distant, was studying his fingertips and ran a wooden match end under the nail of one index finger to remove a speck.

'Madame Lombard is doing well?'

Jef Lombard darted a glance all around, as if seeking something to cling to, then stared at the stove and stammered, 'Very well . . . Thank you.'

By the wall clock behind the counter, Maigret counted five whole minutes without anyone saying a word.

Van Damme, who had let his cigar go out, was the only man who allowed his face to burn with undisguised hatred.

Lombard was the most interesting one to observe. Everything that had happened that day had surely rubbed his nerves raw, and even the tiniest muscle in his face was twitching.

The four men were sitting in an absolute oasis of silence in a café where everyone else was loudly chattering away.

'And *belote* again!' crowed a card player on the right.

'High *tierce*,' said a fellow cautiously on the left. 'We're all agreed on that?'

'Three beers! Three!' shouted the waiter.

The whole café was a beehive of noise and activity except for that one table of four, around which an invisible wall seemed to be growing.

Lombard was the one who broke the spell. He'd been chewing on his lower lip when suddenly he leaped to his feet and gasped, 'The hell with it!'

After glancing briefly but piercingly at his companions, he grabbed his hat and coat and, flinging the door violently open, left the café.

'I bet he bursts into tears as soon as he gets off on his own,' said Maigret thoughtfully.

He'd sensed it, that sob of rage and despair swelling inside the man's throat until his Adam's apple quivered.

Turning to Van Damme, who was staring at the marble tabletop, Maigret tossed down half his beer and wiped his lips with the back of his hand.

The atmosphere was the same – but ten times more concentrated – as in the house in Rheims, where the inspector had first imposed himself on these three people. And the man's imposing bulk itself helped make his stubborn presence all the more menacing.

Maigret was tall and wide, particularly broad-shouldered, solidly built, and his run-of-the-mill clothes emphasized his peasant stockiness. His features were coarse, and his eyes could seem as still and dull as a cow's. In this he resembled certain figures out of children's nightmares, those monstrously big blank-faced creatures that bear down upon sleepers as if to crush them. There was something implacable and inhuman about him that suggested a pachyderm plodding inexorably towards its goal.

He drank his beer, smoked his pipe, watched with satisfaction as the minute hand of the café clock snapped onwards with a metallic click. On a livid clock face!

He seemed to be ignoring everyone and yet he kept an eye on the slightest signs of life to either side.

This was one of the most extraordinary hours of his career. For this stand-off lasted almost one hour: exactly fifty-two minutes! A war of nerves.

Although Jef Lombard had been *hors de combat* practically from the outset, the other two men were hanging on.

Maigret sat between them like a judge, but one who made no accusations and whose thoughts could not be divined. What did he know? Why had he come? What was he waiting for? A word, a gesture that would corroborate his suspicions? Had he already found out the whole truth – or was his confident manner simply a bluff?

And what could anyone say? More musings on coincidence and chance encounters?

Silence reigned. They waited even without any idea of what they were waiting for. They were waiting for something, and nothing was happening!

With each passing minute, the hand on the clock quivered as the mechanism within creaked faintly. At first no one had paid any attention. Now, the sound was incredibly loud – and the event had even separated into three stages: an initial click; the minute hand beginning to move; then another click, as if to slide the hand into its new slot. And as an obtuse angle slowly became an acute angle, the clock face changed: the two hands would eventually meet.

The waiter kept looking over at this gloomy table in

astonishment. Every once in a while, Maurice Belloir would swallow – and Maigret would know this without even looking. He could hear him live, breathe, wince, carefully shift his feet a little now and again, as if he were in church.

Not too many customers were left. The red cloths and playing cards were vanishing from the pale marble table-tops. The waiter stepped outside to close the shutters, while the *patronne* sorted the chips into little piles, according to their value.

'You're staying?' Belloir finally asked, in an almost unrecognizable voice.

'And you?'

'I'm . . . not sure.'

Then Van Damme tapped the table sharply with a coin and called to the waiter, 'How much?'

'For the round? Nine francs seventy-five.'

The three of them were standing now, avoiding one another's eyes, and the waiter helped each of them in turn into his overcoat.

'Goodnight, gentlemen.'

It was so foggy outside that the streetlamps were almost lost in the mist. All the shutters were closed. Somewhere in the distance, footsteps echoed along the pavement.

There was a moment's hesitation, for none of the men wanted to take responsibility for deciding in which direction they would go. Behind them, someone was locking the doors of the café and setting the security bars in place.

Off to the left lay an alley of crookedly aligned old houses.

'Well, gentlemen,' announced Maigret at last, 'the time has come to wish you goodnight.'

He shook Belloir's hand first; it was cold, trembling. The hand Van Damme grudgingly extended was clammy and soft.

The inspector turned up the collar of his overcoat, cleared his throat and began walking alone down the deserted street. And all his senses were attuned to a single purpose: to perceive the faintest noise, the slightest ruffle in the air that might warn him of any danger.

His right hand gripped the butt of the revolver in his pocket. He had the impression that in the network of alleys laid out on his left, enclosed within the centre of Liège like a small island of lepers, people were trying to hurry along without making a sound.

He could just make out a low murmur of conversation but couldn't tell whether it was very near or far away, because the fog was muffling his senses.

Abruptly, he pitched to one side and flattened himself against a door just as a sharp report rang out – and someone, off in the night, took to his heels.

Advancing a few steps, Maigret peered down the alley from which the shot had come but saw only some dark blotches that probably led into blind side alleys and, at the far end 200 metres away, the frosted-glass globe announcing a shop selling *pommes frites*.

A few moments later, as he was walking past that shop, a girl emerged from it with a paper cone of golden *frites*. After propositioning him for form's sake, she headed off to a brighter street.

Grinding the pen-nib down on to the paper with his enormous index finger, Maigret was peacefully writing, pausing from time to time to tamp down the hot ashes in his pipe.

He was ensconced in his room in the Hôtel du Chemin de Fer and according to the illuminated station clock, which he could see from his window, it was two in the morning.

Dear old Lucas,

As one never knows what may happen, I'm sending you the following information so that, if necessary, you will be able to carry on the inquiry I have begun.

1. Last week, in Brussels, a shabbily dressed man who looks like a tramp wraps up thirty thousand-franc notes and sends the package to his own address, Rue de la Roquette, in Paris. The evidence will show that he often sent himself similar sums but that *he did not make any use of the money himself.* The proof is that charred remains of large amounts of banknotes burned on purpose have been found in his room.

He goes by the name of Louis Jeunet and is more or less regularly employed by a workshop on his street.

He is married (contact Mme Jeunet, herbalist, Rue Picpus) and has a child. After some acute episodes of alcoholism, however, he leaves his wife and child under mysterious and troubling circumstances.

In Brussels, after posting the money, he buys a suitcase in which to transport some things he's been keeping in a hotel room. While he is on his way to Bremen, I replace his suitcase with another.

Then Jeunet, *who does not appear to have been contemplating suicide and who has already bought something for his supper,* kills himself upon realizing that the contents of his suitcase have been stolen.

The stolen property is an old suit that does not belong

to him and which, years earlier, had been torn as if in a struggle and drenched with blood. This suit *was made in Liège*.

In Bremen, a man comes to view the corpse: Joseph Van Damme, an import-export commission agent, *born in Liège*.

In Paris, I learn that Louis Jeunet is in reality Jean Lecocq d'Arneville, *born in Liège*, where he studied to graduate level. He disappeared from Liège about ten years ago and no one there has had any news of him, but he has no black marks against his name.

2. In Rheims, before he leaves for Brussels, Jean Lecocq d'Arneville is observed one night entering the home of Maurice Belloir, deputy director of a local bank and *born in Liège*, who denies this allegation.

But the thirty thousand francs sent from Brussels were supplied by this same Belloir.

At Belloir's house I encounter: Van Damme, who has flown in from Bremen; Jef Lombard, a photoengraver *in Liège*; and Gaston Janin, who was also born *in that city*.

As I am travelling back to Paris with Van Damme, he tries to push me into the Marne.

And I find him again *in Liège*, in the home of Jef Lombard, who was an active painter around ten years ago and has covered the walls of his home with works from that period depicting hanged men.

When I consult the local newspaper archives, I find that all the papers of 15 February in the year of the hanged men have been stolen by Van Damme.

That evening, an unsigned letter promises to tell me everything and gives me an appointment in a local café. There I find not one man, but three: Belloir (in from Rheims), Van Damme and Jef Lombard.

They are not pleased to see me. I have the feeling that it's one of these men who has decided to talk; the others seem to be there simply to prevent this.

Lombard cracks under the strain and leaves abruptly. I stay with the other two men. Shortly past midnight, I take leave of them outside, in the fog, and a few moments later a shot is fired at me.

I conclude both that one of the three tried to talk to me and that one of the same three tried to eliminate me.

And clearly, given that this last action amounts to a confession, *the person in question has no recourse but to try again and not miss me.*

But who is it? Belloir, Van Damme, Lombard?

I'll find out when he tries again. Since accidents do happen, I'm sending you these notes on the off chance, so that you will be familiar with the inquiry from the very beginning.

To see the human side of this case, look in particular at Mme Jeunet and Armand Lecocq d'Arneville, the dead man's brother.

And now I'm going to bed. Give my best to everybody back there.

Maigret

The fog had faded away, leaving beads of pearly hoarfrost on the trees and every blade of grass in Square d'Avroy. A chilly sun gleamed in the pale-blue sky as Maigret crossed the square, and with each passing minute the melting frost fell in limpid drops to the gravel.

It was eight in the morning when the inspector strode through the still-deserted Carré, where the folded sandwich boards of film posters stood propped against closed shutters.

When Maigret stopped at a mailbox to post his letter

to Sergeant Lucas, he took a moment to look around him and felt a pang at the thought that somewhere in the city, in those streets bathed in sunlight, a man was at that very moment thinking about him, a man whose salvation depended upon killing him. And the man had the home-ground advantage over the inspector, as he had proved the night before by vanishing into the maze of alleys.

He knew Maigret, too, and was perhaps even watching him where he stood, whereas the inspector did not know who he was.

Could he be Jef Lombard? Did the danger lie in the ramshackle house in Rue Hors-Château, where a woman and her newborn lay sleeping upstairs, watched over by her loving old mother, while her husband's employees worked nonchalantly among the acid baths, hustled along by bicycle messengers from the newspapers?

Joseph Van Damme, a bold, moody and aggressive man, always scheming: was he not lying in wait for the inspector in a place *where he knew Maigret would eventually appear*?

Because that fellow had foreseen everything ever since Bremen! Three lines in a German newspaper – and he showed up at the morgue! He had lunch with Maigret and then beat him to Rheims!

And beat him again to Rue Hors-Château! Beat the investigator to the newspaper archives!

He was even at the Café de la Bourse!

True, there was nothing to prove that he was the one who had decided to talk to Maigret. But there was nothing to prove that he wasn't!

Perhaps it was Maurice Belloir, so cold and formal, the haughty provincial *grand bourgeois*, who had taken a shot at him in the fog. Maybe he was the one whose only hope was to polish off Maigret.

Or Gaston Janin, the little sculptor with the goatee: he hadn't been at the Café de la Bourse, but he could have been lying in ambush in the street . . .

And what connected all that to a hanged man swinging from a church-steeple cross? Or to clusters of hanged men? Or to forests of trees that bore no fruit but hanged men? Or to an old bloodstained suit with lapels clawed by desperate fingernails?

Typists were going off to work. A municipal street sweeper rolled slowly past, its double-nozzle sprayer and brush roller pushing rubbish into the gutter. At street corners, the local police in their white enamel helmets directed traffic with their shiny white gauntlets.

'Police headquarters?' Maigret inquired.

He followed the directions and arrived while the cleaning ladies were still busy, but a cheerful clerk welcomed his French colleague and, upon the inspector's request to examine some ten-year-old police records, but only for the month of February, the man exclaimed in surprise: 'You're the second person in twenty-four hours! You want to know if a certain Joséphine Bollant was in fact arrested for domestic larceny back then, right?'

'Someone came here?'

'Yesterday, towards five in the afternoon. A citizen of Liège who's made it big abroad even though he's still quite a young man! His father was a doctor, and him, he's got a fine business going, in Germany.'

'Joseph Van Damme?'

'The very man! But no matter how hard he looked, he couldn't find what he wanted.'

'Would you show me?'

It was a green index-book of daily reports bound in numerical order. Five entries were listed for 15 February: two for drunkenness and breach of the peace at night, one for shoplifting, one for assault and battery and the last one for breach of close and stealing rabbits.

Maigret didn't bother to look at them. He simply checked the numbers at the top of each form.

'Did Monsieur Van Damme consult the book himself?'

'Yes. He took it into the office next door.'

'Thank you!'

The five reports were numbered 237, 238, 239, 241 and 242.

In other words, number 240 was missing and had been torn out just as the archived newspapers had been ripped from their bindings.

A few minutes later, Maigret was standing in the square behind the town hall, where cars were pulling up to deliver a wedding party. In spite of himself, he was straining to catch the faintest sound, unable to shake a slight feeling of anxiety that he didn't like at all.

8. Little Klein

He had made it just in time: it was nine o'clock. The
employees of the town hall were arriving for work, cross-
ing the main courtyard there and pausing a moment to
greet one another on the handsome stone steps, at the top
of which a doorkeeper with a braided cap and nicely
groomed beard was smoking his pipe.

It was a meerschaum. Maigret noticed this detail, without knowing why; perhaps because it was glinting in the
morning sun, because it looked well seasoned and because
for a moment the inspector envied this man who was
smoking in voluptuous little puffs, standing there as a
symbol of peace and joie de vivre.

For that morning the air was like a tonic that grew more
bracing as the sun rose higher into the sky. A delightful
cacophony reigned, of people shouting in a Walloon dia-
lect, the shrill clanging of the red and yellow streetcars,
and the splashing of the four jets in the monumental
Perron Fountain doing its best to be heard over the hubbub
of the surrounding Place du Marché.

And when Maigret happened to see Joseph Van Damme
head up one side of the double staircase leading to the main
lobby, he hurried after him. Inside the building, the two
staircases continued up on opposite sides, reuniting on each
floor. On one landing, the two men found themselves face
to face, panting from their exertion, struggling to appear

perfectly at ease before the usher with his silver chain of office.

What happened next was short and swift. A question of precision, of split-second timing.

While dashing up the stairs, Maigret had realized that Van Damme had come only to make something disappear, as he had at police headquarters and the newspaper archives.

One of the police reports for 15 February had already been torn out. But in most cities, didn't the police send a copy of all daily reports to the mayor the next morning?

'I would like to see the town clerk,' announced Maigret, with Van Damme only two steps behind him. 'It's urgent . . .'

Their eyes met. They hesitated. The moment for shaking hands passed. When the usher turned expectantly to the businessman from Bremen, he simply murmured, 'It's nothing, I'll come back later.'

He left. The sound of his footsteps died away as he crossed the lobby downstairs.

Shortly afterwards, Maigret was shown into an opulent office, where the town clerk – ramrod straight in his morning coat and a *very* high collar – quickly began the search for the ten-year-old daily police reports.

The room was warm, the carpets soft and springy. A sunbeam lit up a bishop's crozier in a historical painting that took up one whole section of wall.

After half an hour's hunting and a few polite exchanges, Maigret found the reports about the stolen rabbits, the public drunkenness, the shoplifting and then, between two minor incidents, the following lines:

Officer Lagasse, of Division No. 6, was proceeding this morning at six o'clock to the Pont des Arches to take up his post there when, on passing the main door of the Church of Saint-Pholien, he observed a body hanging from the door knocker.

A doctor was immediately summoned but could only confirm the death of the young man, one Émile Klein, born in Angleur, twenty years old, a house painter living in Rue du Pot-au-Noir.

Klein had hanged himself, apparently around the middle of the night, with the aid of a window-blind cord. His pockets held only a few items of no value and some small change.

The inquiry established that the deceased had not been regularly employed for three months, and he seems to have been driven to his action by destitution.

His mother, Madame Klein, a widow who lives in Angleur on a modest pension, has been notified.

There followed hours of feverish activity. Maigret vigorously pursued this new line of inquiry and yet, without being really aware of it, he was less interested in finding out about Klein than he was in finding Van Damme.

For only then, when he had the businessman again in his sights, would he be closing in on the truth. Hadn't it all started in Bremen? And from then on, whenever Maigret scored a point, hadn't he come up against Van Damme?

Van Damme, who had seen him at the town hall, now knew that he'd read the report, that he was tracking down Klein.

At Angleur, nothing! The inspector had taken a taxi deep into an industrial area where small working-class houses, all cast from the same mould in the same sooty grey, lined up on dismal streets at the feet of factory chimneys.

A woman was washing the doorstep of one such house, where Madame Klein had lived.

'It's at least five years since she passed away.'

Van Damme would not be skulking around that neighbourhood.

'Didn't her son live with her?'

'No! And he made a bad end of it: he did away with himself, at the door of a church.'

That was all. Maigret learned only that Klein's father had been a foreman in a coalfield and that after his death his wife lived off a small pension, occupying only a garret in the house, which she sublet.

'To Police Division No. 6,' he told the taxi driver.

As for Officer Lagasse, he was still alive, but he hardly remembered anything.

'It had rained the whole night, he was soaked, and his red hair was sticking to his face.'

'He was tall? Short?'

'Short, I'd say.'

Maigret went next to the gendarmerie, spending almost an hour in offices that smelled of leather and horse sweat.

'If he was twenty years old at the time, he must have been seen by an army medical board . . . Did you say Klein, with a K?'

They found Form 13, in the 'registrant not acceptable' file, and Maigret copied down the information: *height* 1.55 metres, *chest* .80 metres, and a note mentioning 'weak lungs'.

But Van Damme had still not shown up. Maigret had to look elsewhere. The only result of that morning's inquiries was the certainty that clothing B had never belonged to the hanged man of Saint-Pholien, who had been just a shrimp.

Klein had killed himself. There had been no struggle, not a drop of blood shed.

So what tied him to the Bremen tramp's suitcase and the suicide of Lecocq d'Arneville, alias Louis Jeunet?

'Drop me off here . . . And tell me how to find Rue Pot-au-Noir.'

'Behind the church, the street that runs down to Quai Sainte-Barbe.'

After paying off his taxi in front of Saint-Pholien, Maigret took a good look at the new church standing alone in a vast stretch of waste land.

To the right and left of it were boulevards lined by apartment houses built at about the same time as the present church, but behind it there still remained part of the old neighbourhood the city had cut into to make room for Saint-Pholien.

In a stationery shop window, Maigret found some post-cards showing the old church, which had been lower, squatter and completely black. One wing had been shored up with timbers. On three sides, dumpy, mean little houses backed up against its walls and gave the whole place a medieval look.

Nothing was left of this Court of Miracles except a sprawl of old houses threaded with alleys and dead ends, all giving off a nauseating odour of poverty.

A stream of soapy water was running down the middle of Rue du Pot-au-Noir, which wasn't even two paces wide. Kids were playing on the doorsteps of houses teeming with life. And although the sun was shining brightly, its rays could not reach down into the alley. A cooper busy hooping barrels had a brazier burning right out in the street.

The house numbers had worn away, so the inspector had to ask for directions to number 7, which turned out to be all the way down a blind alley echoing with the whine of saws and planes, a workshop with a few carpenter's benches at which three men were labouring away. All the shop doors were open, and some glue was heating on a stove.

Looking up, one of the men put down his dead cigarette butt and waited for the visitor to speak.

'Is this the place where a man named Klein used to live?'

The man glanced knowingly at his companions, pointed to the open door of a dark staircase and grumbled, 'Upstairs! Someone's already there.'

'A new tenant?'

The man gave an odd little smile, which Maigret would understand only later.

'Go see for yourself . . . On the first floor, you can't miss it: there's only the one door . . .'

One of the other workmen shook with silent laughter as he worked his long, heavy plane. Maigret started up the stairs, but after a few steps there was no more banister, and the stairwell was completely shrouded in darkness. He struck a match and saw up ahead a door with no lock or doorknob, and only a string to secure it to a rusty nail.

With his hand in his revolver pocket, Maigret nudged the door open with his knee – and was promptly dazzled by light pouring in from a bay window missing a good third of its panes, a sight so surprising that, when he looked around, it took him a few moments to actually focus on anything.

Finally he noticed, off in a corner, a man leaning against the wall and glowering at him with savage fury: it was Joseph Van Damme.

'We were bound to wind up here, don't you think?' said the inspector, in a voice that resonated strangely in the raw, vacant air of the room.

Saying nothing, staring at him venomously, Van Damme never moved.

To understand the layout of the place, one would have had to know what kind of building – convent, barracks, private house – had once contained these walls, not one of which was smooth or square. And although half the room had wooden flooring, the rest was paved with uneven flagstones, as if it were an old chapel.

The walls were whitewashed, except for a rectangular patch of brown bricks apparently blocking up what had once been a window. The view from the bay window was of a gable, a gutter, and beyond them, some crooked roofs off in the direction of the Meuse.

But by far the most bizarre thing of all was that the place was furnished so incoherently that it might have been a lunatic asylum – or some elaborate practical joke.

Strewn in disorder on the floor were new but unfinished chairs, a door lying flat with one panel repaired, pots of glue, broken saws and crates from which straggled straw or shavings.

Yet off in one corner there was a kind of divan or, rather, a box spring, partly draped with a length of printed calico. And directly overhead hung a slightly battered lantern with coloured glass, the kind sometimes found in second-hand shops.

Separate sections of an incomplete skeleton like the ones medical students use had been tossed on to the divan, but the ribs and the pelvis were still hooked together and sat slumped forward like an old rag doll.

And then there were the walls! White walls, covered with drawings and even painted frescoes that presented perhaps the most arrestingly absurd aspect of the whole room: grinning, grimacing figures and inscriptions along the lines of *Long live Satan, grandfather of the world!*

On the floor lay a bible with a broken back. Elsewhere were crumpled-up sketches and papers yellow with age, all thick with dust.

Over the door, another inscription: *Welcome, damned souls!*

And amid this chaos of junk sat the unfinished chairs, the glue pots, the rough pine planks, smelling like a carpenter's shop. A stove lay on its side, red with rust.

Finally, there was Joseph Van Damme, meticulously groomed in his well-tailored overcoat and impeccable shoes, Van Damme who in spite of everything was still the man-about-town with a modern office at a prestigious address, at home in the great brasseries of Bremen, a lover of fine food and aged Armagnac . . .

. . . Van Damme who called and waved to the leading citizens of Liège from the wheel of his car, remarking that that man in the fur-lined coat was worth millions, that that one over there owned a fleet of thirty merchant ships, Van Damme who would later, serenaded by light music amid the clinking of glasses and saucers, shake the hands of all these magnates with whom he felt a growing fraternity . . .

. . . Van Damme who suddenly looked like a hunted

animal, still frozen with his back against the wall, with white plaster marks on his shoulder and one hand in his overcoat pocket, glaring steadily at Maigret.

'How much?'

Had he really spoken? Could the inspector, in that unreal atmosphere, have been imagining things?

Startled, Maigret knocked over a chair with a caved-in seat, which landed with a loud clatter.

Van Damme had flushed crimson, but not with the glow of health: his hypertensive face betrayed panic – or despair – as well as rage and the desire to live, to triumph at any cost, and he concentrated all his remaining will to resist in his defiant gaze.

'What do you mean?' asked Maigret, going over to the pile of crumpled sketches swept into a corner by the bay window, where he began spreading them out for a look. They were studies of a nude figure, a girl with coarse features, unruly hair, a strong, healthy body with heavy breasts and broad hips.

'There's still time,' Van Damme continued. 'Fifty thousand? . . . A hundred?'

When the inspector gave him a quizzical look, Van Damme, in a fever of ill-concealed anxiety, barked, 'Two hundred thousand!'

Fear shivered in the air within the crooked walls of that miserable room. A bitter, sick, morbid fear.

And perhaps there was something else, too: a repressed desire, the intoxicating temptation of murder . . .

Yet Maigret went on examining the old figure drawings, recognizing in various poses the same voluptuous girl, always staring sullenly into the distance. Once, the artist had tried draping her in the length of calico covering the divan. Another time, he had sketched her in black stockings. Behind her was a skull, which now sat at the foot of the box spring. And Maigret remembered having seen that macabre death's-head in Jef Lombard's self-portrait.

A connection was arising, still only vaguely, among all these people, these events, across time and space. With a faint tremor of excitement, the inspector smoothed out a charcoal sketch depicting a young man with long hair, his shirt collar wide open across his chest and the beginnings of a beard on his chin. He had chosen a Romantic pose: a three-quarter view of the head, and he seemed to be facing the future the way an eagle stares into the sun.

It was Jean Lecocq d'Arneville, the suicide of the sordid hotel in Bremen, the tramp who had never got to eat his last dinner.

'Two hundred thousand francs!'

And the voice added, even now betraying the businessman who thinks of every detail, of the fluctuations in the exchange rate, 'French francs! . . . Listen, inspector . . .'

Maigret sensed that pleading would give way to threats, that the fear quivering in his voice would soon become a growl of rage.

'There's still time, no official action has been taken, and we're in Belgium . . .'

There was a candle end in the lantern; beneath the pile of papers on the floor, the inspector found an old kerosene stove.

'You're not here in an official capacity . . . and even if . . . I'm asking you for a month.'

'Which means it happened in December . . .'

Van Damme seemed to draw back even closer to the wall and stammered, 'What do you mean?'

'It's November now. In February, it will have been ten years since Klein hanged himself, and you're asking me for only one month.'

'I don't understand . . .'

'Oh yes you do!'

And it was maddening, frightening, to see Maigret go on leafing through the old papers with his left hand – and the papers were crackling, rustling – while his right hand remained thrust into his overcoat pocket.

'You understand perfectly, Van Damme! If the problem were Klein's death, and if – for example – he'd been murdered, the statute of limitations would apply only in February, meaning ten years afterwards. Whereas you are asking me for only one month. So *whatever happened . . .* happened in December.'

'You'll never find out anything . . .'

His voice quavered like a wobbly phonograph record.

'Then why are you afraid?'

The inspector lifted up the box spring, underneath which he saw only dust and a greenish, mouldy crust of something barely recognizable as bread.

'Two hundred thousand francs! We could arrange it so that, later on . . .'

'*Do you want me to slap your face?*'

Maigret's threat had been so blunt and unexpected that Van Damme panicked for a moment, raised his arm to protect himself and, in so doing, unintentionally pulled out the revolver he'd been clutching in his coat pocket. Realizing what he'd done, he was again overcome for a few seconds by that intoxicating temptation . . . but must have hesitated to shoot.

'Drop it!'

He let go. The revolver fell to the floor, near a pile of wood shavings.

And, turning his back to the enemy, Maigret kept on rummaging through the bewildering collection of incongruous things. He picked up a yellowish sock, also marbled with mildew.

'So tell me, Van Damme . . .'

Sensing a change in the silence, Maigret turned round and saw the man pass a hand over his face, where his fingers left wet streaks on his cheeks.

'You're crying?'

'*Me*?'

He'd said this aggressively, sardonically, despairingly.

'What branch of the army were you in?'

Van Damme was baffled by the inspector's question, but ready to snatch at any scrap of hope.

'I was in the École des Sous-Lieutenants de Réserve, at Beverloo.'

'Infantry?'

'Cavalry.'

'So you must have been between one metre sixty-five and one metre seventy. And you weren't over seventy kilos. It was later that you put on some weight.'

Maigret pushed away a chair he'd bumped into, then picked up another scrap of paper – it looked like part of a letter – with only a single line on it: *Dear old thing* . . .

But he kept an eye on Van Damme, who was still trying to figure out what Maigret had meant and who – in sudden understanding, his face haggard – cried out in horror, 'It wasn't me! I swear I've never worn that suit!'

Maigret's foot sent Van Damme's revolver spinning to the other side of the room.

Why, at that precise moment, did he count up the children again? A little boy in Belloir's house. Three kids in Rue Hors-Château, and the newest hadn't even opened her eyes yet! Plus the son of the false Louis Jeunet . . .

On the floor, the beautiful naked girl was arching her back, throwing out her chest on an unsigned sketch in red chalk.

There were hesitant footsteps, out on the stairs; a hand fumbled at the door, feeling for the string that served as a latch.

9. The Companions of the Apocalypse

In what happened next, everything mattered: the words, the silences, the looks they gave one another, even the involuntary twitch of a muscle. Everything had great meaning, and there was a sense that behind the actors in these scenes loomed an invisible pall of fear.

The door opened. Maurice Belloir appeared, and his first glance was for Van Damme, over in the corner with his back to the wall. The second glance took in the revolver lying on the floor.

It was enough; he understood. Especially when he saw Maigret, with his pipe, still calmly going through the pile of old sketches.

'Lombard's coming!' announced Belloir, without seeming to address anyone in particular. 'I grabbed a taxi.'

Hearing this was enough to tell Maigret that the bank deputy director had just given up. The evidence was slight: a gentle easing of tension in his face; a hint of shame in his tired voice.

The three of them looked at one another. Joseph Van Damme spoke first.

'What is he . . . ?'

'He's gone crazy. I tried to calm him down, but he got away from me. He went off talking to himself, waving his arms around . . .'

'He has a gun?' asked Maigret.

'He has a gun.'

Maurice Belloir tried to listen carefully, with the strained look of a stunned man struggling in vain to recover control of himself.

'Both of you were down in Rue Hors-Château? Waiting for the result of my conversation with . . .'

He pointed to Van Damme, and Belloir nodded.

'And all three of you agreed to offer me . . . ?'

He didn't need to say everything; they understood right away. They all understood even the silences and felt as if they could hear one another think.

Suddenly footsteps were racing up the stairs. Someone tripped, must have fallen, then moaned with rage. The next moment the door was kicked open and framed the figure of Jef Lombard, stock still for an instant as he gazed at the three men with terrifying intensity.

He was shaking, gripped by fever, perhaps by some kind of insanity.

What he saw must have been a mad vision of Belloir backing away from him, Van Damme's congested face, and then Maigret, broad-shouldered and absolutely immobile, holding his breath.

And there was all that bewildering junk to boot, with the lantern and the broken-down divan and the spread-out drawings covering all but the breasts and chin of the naked girl in that sketch . . .

The scene lasted for mere fractions of a second. Jef Lombard's long arm was holding out a revolver. Maigret watched him quietly. Still, he did heave a sigh when Lombard threw the gun to the floor, grabbed his head with both hands and burst into great raw sobs.

'I can't, I can't!' he groaned. 'You hear me? God damn it, I can't!'

And he turned away to lean both arms against the wall, his shoulders heaving. They could hear him snuffling softly.

The inspector went over and closed the door, to shut off the noise of sawing and planing downstairs and the distant cries of children out in the street.

Jef Lombard wiped his face with his handkerchief, tossed back his hair and looked around with the empty eyes of someone whose nerves have just given way. He was not completely calm; his fingers were flexing like claws, he was breathing heavily, and when he tried to speak he had to bite his lip to suppress the sob welling in his throat.

'To end up like this!' he finally said, his voice dark and biting.

He tried to laugh, but sounded desperate.

'Nine years! Almost ten! I was left all alone, with no money, no job . . .'

He was talking to himself, probably unaware that he was staring hard at the figure drawing of the nude with that bare flesh . . .

'Ten years of slogging away, every day, with difficulties and disappointments of all kinds, but I got married anyway, I wanted kids . . . I drove myself like an animal to give them a decent life. A house! And the workshop! Everything – you saw that! But what you didn't see is what it cost me to build it all, and the *heartbreaks* . . . The bills that kept me awake at night when I was just getting started . . .'

Passing his hand over his forehead, he swallowed hard, and his Adam's apple rose and fell.

'And now look: I've just had a baby girl and I can't remember if I've even seen her! My wife is lying in bed unable to understand what's going on, she sneaks frightened looks at me, she doesn't recognize me any more . . . My men ask me questions, and I don't know what to tell them.

'All gone! Suddenly, in a few days: wrecked, ruined, done for, smashed to pieces! *Everything!* Ten years of work! And all because . . .'

Clenching his fists, he looked down at the gun on the floor, then up at Maigret. He was at the end of his rope.

'Let's get it over with,' he sighed, wearily waving a hand. 'Who's going to do the talking? It's so stupid!'

And he might have been speaking to the skull, the heap of old sketches, the wild, outlandish drawings on the walls.

'Just so stupid . . .'

He seemed on the verge of tears again, but no, he was all done in. The fit had passed. He went over to sit on the edge of the divan, planted his elbows on his bony knees, his chin in his hands, and sat there, waiting.

He moved only to scrape a bit of mud off the bottom of a trouser leg with a fingernail.

'Am I disturbing you?' asked a cheery voice.

The carpenter entered, covered in sawdust, and, after looking around at the drawings decorating the walls, he laughed.

'So, you came back to look at all this?'

No one moved. Only Belloir tried to look as if nothing were wrong.

'Do you remember about those twenty francs you still owe me for that last month? Oh, not that I've come to ask you for them. It just makes me laugh, because when you left without taking all this old junk, I recall you saying, "Maybe one day a single one of these sketches might well be worth as much as this whole dump." I didn't believe you. Still, I did put off whitewashing the walls. One day I brought up a framer who sells pictures and he went off with two or three drawings. Gave me a hundred sous for them. Do you still paint?'

It finally dawned on him that something was wrong. Van Damme was staring stubbornly at the floor. Belloir was impatiently snapping his fingers.

'Aren't you the one who set himself up in Rue Hors-Château?' asked the carpenter, turning to Jef Lombard. 'I've a nephew worked with you. A tall blond fellow . . .'

'Maybe,' sighed Lombard, turning away.

'You I don't recognize. . . Were you with this lot?'

Now the landlord was speaking to Maigret.

'No.'

'What a weird bunch! My wife didn't want me to rent to them, and then she advised me to throw them out, especially since they didn't pay up very often. But they amused me. Always looking to be the one wearing the biggest hat, or smoking the longest clay pipe. And they used to sing together and drink all night long! And some pretty girls would show up sometimes . . . Speaking of which, Monsieur Lombard, that one there, on the floor, do you know what happened to her? . . .

'She married a shop walker at Le Grand Bazar and she lives about two hundred metres down the street from here. She has a son who goes to school with mine . . .'

Lombard stood up, went over to the bay window, and

retraced his steps in such agitation that the carpenter decided to beat a retreat.

'Maybe I am disturbing you after all, so I'll leave you to it. And you know, if you're interested in anything here . . . Of course, I never held on to this stuff on account of the twenty francs! All I took was one landscape, for my dining room.'

Out on the landing, he seemed about to start chatting again, but was summoned from downstairs.

'Someone to see you, *patron!*'

'Later, then, gentlemen. Glad to have met—'

The closing door cut off his voice. Although inopportune, the carpenter's visit had eased some of the tension, and while he'd been talking, Maigret had lit his pipe.

Now he pointed to the most puzzling drawing on the wall, an image encircled by an inscription that read: *The Companions of the Apocalypse.*

'Was this the name of your group?'

Sounding almost like himself again, it was Belloir who replied.

'Yes. I'll explain . . . It's too late for us, isn't it – and tough luck for our wives and children . . .'

But Lombard broke in: 'Let me tell him, I want to . . .'

And he began pacing up and down the room, now and then looking over at some object or other, as if to illustrate his story.

'Just over ten years ago, I was studying painting at the Académie, where I used to go around in a wide-brimmed hat and a *lavallière* . . . Two others there with me were Gaston Janin, who was studying sculpture, and little Émile Klein. We would parade proudly around the

Carré – because we were *artists*, you understand? Each of us thought he'd be at least another Rembrandt!

'It all started so foolishly . . . We read a lot, and favoured the Romantic period. We'd get carried away and idolize some writer for a week, then drop that one and adopt another . . .

'Little Klein, whose mother lived in Angleur, rented this studio we're in, and we started meeting here. We were really impressed by the medieval atmosphere of the neighbourhood, especially on winter evenings. We'd sing old songs and recite Villon's poetry . . .

'I don't remember any more who discovered the Book of Revelation – the Apocalypse of John – and insisted on reading us whole chapters from it.

'One evening we met a few university students: Belloir, Lecocq d'Arneville, Van Damme, and a Jewish fellow named Mortier, whose father has a shop selling tripe and sausage casings not far from here.

'We got to drinking and wound up bringing them back to the studio. The oldest of them wasn't even twenty-two. That was you, Van Damme, wasn't it?'

It was doing Lombard good to talk. His movements were less abrupt, his voice less hoarse, but his face was still blotched with red and his lips swollen from weeping.

'I think it was my idea to found a group, a society! I'd read about the secret societies in German universities during the eighteenth century. A club that would unite Science and Art!'

Looking around the studio walls, he couldn't help sneering.

'Because we were just full of that kind of talk! Hot air

that puffed up our pride. On the one side were Klein, Janin and me, the paint-pushers: we were Art! On the other side, our new university friends. We drank to that. Because we drank a lot ... We drank to feel even more gloriously superior! And we'd dim the lights to create an atmosphere of mystery.

'We'd lounge around right here, look: some of us on the divan, the others on the floor. We'd smoke pipe after pipe, until the air became a thick haze. Then we'd all start singing. There was almost always someone feeling sick who'd have to go and throw up in the courtyard. We'd still be going strong at two, three in the morning, working ourselves up into a frenzy. Helped along by the wine, some cheap rotgut that upset our stomachs, we used to soar off into the realm of metaphysics ...

'I can still see little Klein ... He was the most excitable one, the nervous type. He wasn't well. His mother was poor and he lived on nothing, went without food so he could drink. Because when we'd been drinking, we all felt like real geniuses!

'The university contingent was a little more level-headed, because they weren't as poor, except for Lecocq d'Arneville. Belloir would swipe a bottle of nice old Burgundy or liqueur from his parents, and Van Damme used to bring some charcuterie ...

'We were convinced that people used to look at us out in the street with fear and admiration, and we chose an arcane, sonorous, lofty name: *The Companions of the Apocalypse*. Actually, I don't think any of us had read the Book of Revelation all the way through ... Klein was the only one who could recite a few passages by heart, when he was drunk.

'We'd all decided to split the rent for the room, but Klein was allowed to live here.

'A few girls agreed to come pose for us for free . . . Pose and all the rest, naturally! And we tried to think of them as *grisettes* from *La Bohème*! And all that half-baked folderol . . .

'There's one of the girls, on the floor. Dumb as they come. But we painted her as a Madonna anyway.

'Drinking – that was the main thing. We had to ginger up the atmosphere at all costs. Klein once tried to achieve the same effect by pouring sulphuric ether on the divan. And I remember all of us, working ourselves up, waiting for intoxication, expecting visions . . . Oh God Almighty!'

Lombard went over to cool his forehead against a misty windowpane, but when he came back there was a new quaver in his voice.

'Chasing after this frenzied exaltation, we wound up nervous wrecks – especially those of us who weren't eating enough, you understand? Little Klein, among others: a poor kid going without food to over-stimulate himself with drink . . .

'And it was as if we were rediscovering the world all on our own, naturally! We were full of opinions on every great problem, and full of scorn for society, established truths and everything bourgeois. When we'd had a few drinks and smoked up a storm, we'd spout the most cock-eyed nonsense, a hodgepodge of Nietzsche, Karl Marx, Moses, Confucius, Jesus Christ . . .

'Here's an example: I don't remember which one of us discovered that *pain doesn't exist*, the brain's simply imagining it. One night I became so enthralled with the idea that, surrounded by my excited audience, I stabbed myself in the upper arm with a pocket knife *and forced myself to smile about it*!

'And we had other wild inspirations like that . . . We were an elite, a coterie of geniuses who'd come together by chance and were way above the conventional world with its laws and preconceived opinions. A gathering of the gods, hey? Gods who were sometimes dying of hunger but who strode through the streets with their heads high, crushing passers-by with their contempt.

'And we had the future completely in hand: Lecocq d'Arneville would become a new Tolstoy, while Van Damme, who was taking boring courses at our university business school, would fundamentally redefine economics and upend all the accepted ideas about the social workings of humanity. And each one of us had a role to play, as poets, painters and future heads of state.

'All fuelled by booze! Or just fumes! Because by the end we were so used to flying high here that simply by walking through that door, into the alchemical light of the lantern, with a skeleton in the shadows and the skull we used as a communal drinking bowl, we'd catch the little fever we craved, all on our own.

'Even the most modest among us could already envision the marble plaque that would one day adorn this house: *Here met the famous Companions of the Apocalypse* . . . We all tried to come up with the newest great book or amazing idea. It's a miracle we didn't all wind up anarchists! Because we actually discussed that question, quite seriously. There'd been an incident in Seville; someone read the newspaper article about it aloud, and I don't remember any more who shouted, "True genius is destructive!"

'Well, our kiddy club debated this subject for hours. We

came up with ways to make bombs. We cast about for interesting things to blow up.

'Then little Klein, who was on his sixth or seventh glass, became ill, but not like the other times. This was some kind of nervous fit: he was writhing on the floor, and all we could think of any more was what would happen to us if something happened to him! And that girl was there! Henriette, her name was. She was crying . . .

'Oh, those were some nights, all right . . . It was a point of honour with us not to leave until the lamplighter had turned off the gas streetlamps, and then we'd head out shivering into the dreary dawn. Those of us who were better off would sneak home through a window, sleep, eat and more or less recover from our nightly excesses, but the others – Klein, Lecocq d'Arneville and I – would drag ourselves through the streets, nibbling on a roll and looking longingly into shop windows . . .

'That year I didn't have an overcoat because I wanted to buy a wide-brimmed hat that cost a hundred and twenty francs, and I pretended that, like everything else, cold was an illusion. And primed by all our discussions, I announced to my father, a good, honest man, a gunsmith's assistant – he's dead, now – that parental love is the worst form of selfishness and that a child's first duty is to reject his family.

'He was a widower. He used to go off to work in the morning at six o'clock, just when I was getting home. Well, he took to setting out earlier so he wouldn't run into me, because my big speeches frightened him. And he would leave me little notes on the table: *There's some cold meat in the cupboard. Father* . . .'

★

Lombard's voice broke for a moment. He looked over at Belloir, who was sitting on the edge of a staved-in chair, staring at the floor, and then at Van Damme, who was shredding a cigar to bits.

'There were seven of us,' said Lombard dully. 'Seven supermen! Seven geniuses! Seven kids!

'Janin's still sculpting, off in Paris – or rather, he makes shop-window mannequins for a big factory. Now and then he works off his frustration by doing something from a real model, his mistress of the moment . . . Belloir's in banking, Van Damme's in business, I'm a photoengraver . . .'

The fear in that silent room was now palpable. Lombard swallowed hard but went on, and his eyes seemed to sink even deeper into their dark sockets.

'Klein hanged himself at the church door . . . Lecocq d'Arneville shot himself in the mouth in Bremen . . .'

Another silence. This time, unable to sit still, Belloir stood up, hesitated, then went to stand by the bay window. A strange noise seemed to be rumbling in his chest.

'And the last one?' inquired Maigret. 'Mortier, I believe? The tripe dealer's son.'

Lombard now stared at him so frantically that the inspector thought he might have another fit. Van Damme somehow knocked over a chair.

'It was in December, wasn't it?'

As he was speaking, Maigret kept a close eye on the three men.

'In a month it will have been ten years. The statute of limitations will come into effect.'

He went first to pick up Van Damme's automatic, then collected the revolver Lombard had thrown away after he arrived.

Maigret had seen it coming: Lombard was breaking down, holding his head in his hands and wailing, 'My children! My three little ones!'

And with renewed hysteria, unashamed to show the tears streaming down his face, he yelled, 'It's because of you, you, only because of you, that I haven't even seen my newborn child, my little girl! I couldn't even say what she looks like . . . *Do you understand?*'

10. *Christmas Eve in Rue du Pot-au-Noir*

There must have been a passing shower, some swift low-lying clouds, because all the sunshine glinting off objects in the room vanished in an instant. As if a switch had been flicked, the light turned uniformly grey, while the clutter took on a glum look.

Maigret understood why those who'd gathered there had felt the need to doctor the light with a lantern of many colours, set their stage with mysterious shadows and muddle the atmosphere with drink and tobacco smoke.

And he could imagine how Klein would awaken in the morning after those sad orgies to find himself surrounded by empty bottles, broken glasses and rancid odours, all bathed in the murk from the bay window, which had no curtains.

Jef Lombard was too upset to go on, and it was Maurice Belloir who took up the story.

Everything shifted, as if they'd moved to a different register. Lombard had been shaken to his very core, his emotion expressed through wrenching sobs, shrill, wheezing catches in his voice, nervous pacing and periods of alternating agitation and calm that could have been plotted on a medical chart, while Belloir's entire person – his voice, his gaze, his every move – was under such taut control that it was painful to see, for it clearly demanded a gruelling effort of will and concentration.

This man could never have cried, or even tried to smile: he held himself completely still.

'May I take over, inspector? It will be dark soon and we'll have no light here.'

It was not Belloir's fault that he'd brought up a practical detail, and it wasn't from lack of feeling, for it was actually his own way of showing how he felt.

'I believe that we were all sincere in our arguments and endless discussions, and when we were dreaming out loud. But there were different degrees of sincerity involved.

'Jef has mentioned this. On the one hand, there were the wealthy ones, who went home afterwards to recover their balance in a stable environment: Van Damme, Willy Mortier and I. And even Janin, who had everything he needed.

'Willy Mortier was in a class by himself, however. A case in point: he was the only one who chose his mistresses from among professional nightclub singers and the dancers in second-rate theatres. He paid them.

'He was a practical, unsentimental person, like his father, who arrived in Liège with empty pockets, matter-of-factly chose the sausage-casing business – and made a fortune.

'Willy received a monthly allowance of 500 francs, which seemed a fabulous sum to the rest of us. He never set foot inside the university, paid poorer students to take notes for him in lectures and "arranged" to pass his exams through favours and bribes.

'He came here simply out of curiosity, because he never shared our tastes or ideas. Look at his father: he'd buy paintings from artists even though he despised them, and he "bought" city councilmen and even aldermen as well, to get what he wanted. He despised them, too.

'Well, Willy despised us in the same way. He was a rich boy who came here to see just how different he was from the rest of us.

'He didn't drink. And those who got drunk here disgusted him. During our epic discussions, he'd say only a few words, but they were like ice water, the kind of words that hurt because they're too blunt, because they ruined the fake poetic atmosphere we'd managed to create.

'He hated us! And we hated him! On top of everything else, he was stingy – and cynical about it. Klein didn't always get something to eat every day, so one or the other of us would help him out now and then. Mortier? He'd announce, "I don't want any difficulties about money to come between us. I don't want to be welcomed simply because I'm well off."

'And he'd cough up *exactly* his share when we were all turning our pockets inside out to buy something to drink.

'It was Lecocq d'Arneville who used to take lecture notes for him, and I once overheard Willy refuse to give him an advance on his payment.

'He was the alien, hostile element that crops up almost every time when men get together. We put up with him. Klein, though, when he was drunk, used to attack him savagely, really let everything that bothered him come pouring out. Mortier would go a bit pale bur he'd just listen, with a faint sneer . . .

'I mentioned various kinds of sincerity. Klein and Lecocq d'Arneville were definitely the most forthright, unpretentious members of our group. They were close, like brothers. They'd both had difficult childhoods, with their mothers watching every sou . . . Both these fellows were desperate to better themselves and agonized over anything that stood in their way.

'Klein had to work during the day as a house painter to pay for his evening classes at the Académie, and he did tell us that it made him dizzy when he had to climb a ladder. Lecocq took lecture notes for others, gave French lessons to foreign students; he often came here to eat. The stove must still be around here somewhere . . .'

It was lying on the floor near the divan, where Lombard gave it a gloomy kick.

Not one hair was out of place on Maurice Belloir's sleek head, and his voice was flat, stripped down.

'Since those days, I've heard people in the middle-class drawing rooms of Rheims ask jokingly, "In such-and-such a situation, would you be able to kill someone?" Sometimes it's the mandarin question, you know the one: *If all you had to do was push a button to kill a wealthy mandarin way off in China to inherit his riches, would you do it?*

'We took up the weirdest ideas here and talked for nights on end, so we inevitably came around to the enigma of life and death . . .

'It was almost Christmas; it had been snowing. A short item in a newspaper started us off. We always had to challenge the status quo, right? So we went all out on this idea: mankind is just a patch of mould on the earth's crust. So human life and death don't matter, pity is only a sickness, big animals eat the little ones, and we eat the big ones.

'Lombard told you about the pocket knife: stabbing himself to prove that pain didn't exist!

'Well, that night, shortly before Christmas, with three or four empty bottles lying around on the floor, we seriously debated the idea of killing someone. After all, weren't we off in the realm of pure theory, where anything goes? All bright-eyed, we kept quizzing one another with shivers of guilty excitement.

'"Would *you* be brave enough?"

'"Why not? If life is nothing, just some accident, a blemish on the face of the earth . . . "

'"A stranger, passing in the street?"

'And Klein – so pale, with those dark rings under his eyes – he'd drunk the most. And he yelled, "Yes!"

'We were afraid to take another step: it felt like being at the edge of a cliff. We were dicing with danger, joking around with this murder we'd conjured up, and now that murder seemed to be stalking *us* . . .

'Someone who'd been an altar boy – I think it was Van Damme – started singing the *Libera nos*, which the priest chants over a coffin, and we all took up the chorus, playing this ghoulish game with real relish.

'But we didn't kill anyone that night! At four a.m. I went over the garden wall to sneak home. By eight I was having coffee with my family. The whole thing was only a memory, you understand? Like remembering being scared watching a play in a theatre.

'But Klein stayed here, at Rue du Pot-au-Noir, where all those ideas kept seething in his sickly, swollen head. They were eating him alive. We could tell what was worrying him from the questions he kept popping at us over the next few days.

'"Do you really think it's hard to kill someone?"

'We weren't drunk any more but we didn't want to

back down, so we blustered, we said, "Of course it isn't!"

'Maybe we were even getting a thrill out of his childish excitement, but get this straight: we had no intention of causing a tragedy! We were still seeing how far we could go . . .

'When there's a fire, onlookers can't help wanting it to last, to be a *spectacular* fire, and when the river is rising, newspaper readers hope for *major* flooding they can talk about for the next twenty years. *They want something interesting, and it doesn't matter what!*

'Christmas Eve arrived. Everybody brought some bottles. We drank, we sang, and Klein, already half-soused, kept pulling one after another of us aside.

'"Do you think I'd be able to kill someone?"

'We weren't worried about it. By midnight no one was sober. We talked about going out for more bottles.

'That's when Willy Mortier showed up, in a dinner jacket, with a broad white shirt front that seemed to soak up all the light. His face was rosy, he was wearing scent, and he announced that he'd just come from a fancy society reception.

'"Go and get some booze!" Klein yelled at him.

'"You're drunk, chum! I just came along to pay my respects."

'"No, to look down your nose at us!"

'There still wasn't any reason to suspect that something might happen, although Klein's face was more frightening than it had ever been during his other drunken spells. He was so small, so thin next to the other man . . . His hair was a mess, his forehead was all sweaty, and he'd yanked his tie off.

'"Klein," said Willy, "you're stinking drunk!"'

'"So what! This stinking drunk's telling you to go and get some booze!"'

'I think that scared Willy. He'd begun to sense that this was no laughing matter, but he still tried to bluff his way out . . . His black hair had been curled and perfumed . . .

'"You fellows don't seem to be having much fun here," he told us. "It was livelier back with the stuffed shirts I just left!"

'"Go and get some booze . . ."

'Now Klein was circling him, staring at him, all wound up. A few of us were off in a corner, talking about some Kantian theory or other. Someone else was weeping and swearing that he wasn't fit to live.

'Not one of us had all his wits about him, and no one saw the whole thing: Klein darting forward abruptly, a furious little bundle of nerves, and striking Mortier . . .

'It looked as if he'd butted him in the chest with his head, but we saw blood spurting out! Willy opened his mouth so wide . . .'

'No!' Lombard begged suddenly, now standing and staring at Belloir as if in a daze.

Van Damme had retreated back to the wall, his shoulders slumping. But nothing could have stopped Belloir, not even if he had wanted to himself. It was growing dark. Everyone's face looked grey.

'We were all frantic!' the voice went on. 'And Klein huddled there with a knife in his hand, stunned, gaping at Willy, who just stood swaying, tottering . . . These things don't happen the way people imagine – I can't explain . . .

'Mortier was still on his feet in spite of the blood streaming from the hole in his shirt front. He said – and I'm sure of this – "Bastards!" And he kept standing in the same place, his legs slightly apart, as if to keep his balance. If he hadn't been bleeding, you'd have thought *he* was the drunk.

'He had big eyes, and now they seemed even bigger . . . His left hand was clutching the button of his dinner jacket, while his right was fumbling around the back of his trousers.

'Someone – I think it was Jef – shouted in terror, and we saw Mortier's right hand pull a revolver slowly from a pocket, a small black thing, made of steel, that looked so *hard* . . .

'Klein was rolling on the floor in a fit. A bottle fell, smashing into pieces.

'And Willy was still alive! Just barely swaying, he looked at us, one after the other! Although he couldn't have been seeing clearly . . . He raised the revolver . . .

'Then someone stepped forwards to grab the gun from him, slipped in the blood, and the two of them fell to the floor.

'Mortier must have gone into convulsions – because he still wasn't dead, you hear me? His eyes, those big eyes, were wide open! He kept trying to shoot, and he said it again: "Bastards!"

'The other man's hand was able to grip his throat . . . He hadn't much longer to live, anyway . . .

'*I got completely soaked . . . while the dinner jacket just lay there on the floor.*'

★

Van Damme and Lombard were now looking at their companion in horror. And Belloir finished what he had to say.

'That hand around his neck, it was mine! I was the man who slipped in that pool of blood . . .'

He was standing in the same place as he had then. Now, though, he was dapper and soigné, his shoes polished, his suit impeccable. He wore a large gold signet ring on his white, well-cared-for hand with its manicured nails.

'We were in a state of shock. We made Klein go to bed, even though he wanted to go and give himself up. No one spoke. Again, I can't explain . . . And yet I was quite lucid! I'll say it again: people don't understand what such tragedies are really like. I dragged Van Damme out on to the landing, where we talked quietly, while Klein kept howling and struggling.

'The church bells rang the hour while three of us were going down the alley carrying the body, but I don't remember what time it was. The Meuse was in spate – Quai Sainte-Barbe was under half a metre of water – and the current was running fast. Both upstream and down, the barrage gates were open. We just caught a glimpse of a dark mass being swept past the nearest lamp post by the rushing water.

'My suit was stained and torn; I left it at the studio after Van Damme went home to get me some of his clothes. The next day, I concocted a story for my parents . . .'

'Did you all get together again?' Maigret asked slowly.

'No. Most of us bolted from Rue du Pot-au-Noir. Lecocq d'Arneville stayed on with Klein. And ever since then, we've all avoided one another, as if by mutual agreement. Whenever any of us met up by accident in town, we looked the other way.

'It turned out that Willy's body was never found, thanks to the flood. Since he hadn't been proud of knowing us, he'd always been careful never to mention us at home. People thought he'd simply run off for a few days. Later, they did look for him in the seedy parts of town, where they thought he might have finished up that evening.

'I was the first to leave Liège, three weeks later. I suddenly broke off my studies and announced to my family that I wanted to pursue my career in France. I found work in a bank in Paris.

'I learned from the newspapers that Klein had hanged himself that February at the door of Saint-Pholien.

'One day I ran into Janin, in Paris. We didn't talk about the tragedy, but he told me that he, too, had moved to France.'

'I stayed on in Liège, alone,' muttered Lombard resentfully, his head hanging.

'You drew hanged men and church steeples,' Maigret said. 'Then you did sketches for the newspapers. Then . . .'

And he recalled the house in Rue Hors-Château, the windows with the small, green-tinged panes, the fountain in the courtyard, the portrait of the young woman, the photoengraving workshop, where posters and magazine illustrations were gradually invading the walls of hanged men . . .

And the kids! The newest one born only yesterday . . .

Hadn't ten years gone by? And little by little, more or less clumsily, hadn't life returned to normal everywhere?

Van Damme had roamed around Paris, like the other two. By chance, he'd wound up in Germany. His parents had left him an inheritance. He had become an important businessman in Bremen.

Maurice Belloir had made a fine marriage. Moving up the ladder, he was now a bank deputy director! Then there was the lovely new house in Rue de Vesle, where a little boy was studying the violin.

In the evening he played billiards with other town luminaries in the comfortable ambience of the Café de Paris.

Janin got by with a series of mistresses, earned his living by making shop-window mannequins and relaxed by working on portrait busts of his lady friends.

And hadn't even Lecocq d'Arneville got married? Didn't his wife and child live in the back of the herbalist's shop in Rue Picpus?

Willy Mortier's father was still buying, cleaning and selling whole truckloads of pig's entrails, bribing city councilmen and growing ever richer.

His daughter had married a cavalry officer, who hadn't wanted to join the family business, whereupon Mortier had refused to hand over the agreed-upon dowry.

The couple lived off somewhere in a small garrison town.

11. The Candle End

It was nearly dark. Their faces were receding into the shadows, but their features seemed all the more sharply etched.

Lombard was the one who burst out, as if alarmed by the gathering dusk, 'We need some light!'

There was still a candle end, left in the lantern that had hung from the same nail for ten years, kept along with the broken-down divan, the length of calico, the battered skeleton, the sketches of the girl with naked breasts and everything else saved as security by the landlord still waiting for his rent.

When Maigret lit the stump, shadows danced on the walls, which shone red, yellow and blue in light glowing through the tinted glass panes, as if from a magic lantern.

'When did Lecocq d'Arneville come to see you for the first time?' the inspector asked, turning towards Belloir.

'It must be about three years ago. I hadn't been expecting it . . . The house you saw had just been finished. My boy was barely walking yet.

'I was struck by how much he'd grown to resemble Klein: not so much physically as in his nature. That same feverish intensity, the same morbid uneasiness. He came as an enemy. He was furious and embittered, or desperate – I can't find exactly the right word. He sniggered at me, spoke aggressively, he was on edge; he pretended to admire

my home, my position, my life and character, and yet . . .
I had the feeling he might burst into tears, like Klein when
he was drunk!

'He thought that I'd forgotten. Not true! I simply
wanted to live, you understand me? And that's why I
worked like a dog: to live . . .

'But he hadn't been able to get on with his life. He had
lived with Klein for two months after that Christmas Eve,
it's true . . . We left, they stayed behind: the two of them,
here in this room, in . . .

'I can't explain what I felt in his presence. So many years
had passed, but I had the feeling Lecocq d'Arneville had
remained exactly the same. It was as if life had moved on
for some, and stopped short for others.

'He told me that he'd changed his name because he
didn't want to keep anything that reminded him of that
awful night. He'd even changed his life! He'd never opened
another book. He'd got it into his head to build a new life
by becoming a manual labourer.

'I had to glean all this information on my own, weeding
it out from all his reproaches, caustic remarks and truly
monstrous accusations.

'He'd failed! Been a disaster at everything! And part of
him was still rooted right here. It was the same for the rest
of us, I think, but in our case it was less intense, not as
painful, as unhealthy. I believe Klein's face haunted him
even more than Willy's did.

'Married, with a kid, he'd been through some tough
times and had turned to drink. He was unable, not only
to be happy, but even to be at any kind of peace. He
screamed at me that he adored his wife and had left her
because when he was near her, he felt like a thief! A thief

stealing happiness! Happiness stolen from Klein . . . And the other man.

'You see, I've thought a lot about this since then. And I think I understand. We were fooling around with dangerous ideas, with mysticism and morbid thoughts. It was only a game, and we were just kids, playing, but at least two of us let themselves fall into the trap. The most excitable, fanatical ones.

'Klein and Lecocq d'Arneville. We'd all talked about killing someone? Klein went on to do it! And then he killed himself! And Lecocq, appalled, a broken man, was chained to this nightmare for the rest of his life.

'The others and I tried to escape, to find our way back to a normal life, whereas Lecocq d'Arneville threw himself recklessly into his remorse, in a rage of despair. He destroyed his own life! Along with those of his wife and son . . .

'So he turned on us. Because that's why he'd come looking for me. I hadn't understood that at first. He looked around at *my* house, *my* family, *my* bank. And I really did feel that he considered it his duty to destroy all that.

'To avenge Klein! To avenge himself.

'He threatened me. He had kept the suit, with the rips, the bloodstains, and it was the only physical proof of what happened that Christmas Eve. He asked me for money. Lots of it! And asked for more later on.

'Because wasn't that where we were vulnerable? Van Damme, Lombard, myself, even Janin: everything we had achieved depended on money.

'It was the beginning of a new nightmare! Lecocq had known what he was doing, and he went from one to another of us, lugging along that sinister ruined suit. With diabolical cunning, he calculated precisely how much to ask us for, to make us feel the pinch.

'You saw my house, inspector. It's mortgaged! My wife thinks her dowry is sitting untouched at the bank, but there's not a centime of it left. And I've done other things like that.

'He went twice to Bremen, to see Van Damme. He came to Liège. Still consumed with fury, bent on destroying every last scrap of happiness.

'There were six of us around Willy's corpse. Klein was dead; Lecocq was trapped in a living nightmare. So we all had to be equally miserable. And he didn't even spend the money! He lived as wretchedly as before, when he was sharing a bit of cheap sausage with Klein. He burned all the money! And every banknote he burned meant unbelievable hardship for us all.

'For three years we've been struggling, each off in his own corner: Van Damme in Bremen, Jef in Liège, Janin in Paris, myself in Rheims. For three years we've hardly dared write to one another, while Lecocq d'Arneville was forcing us back into the madness of the Companions of the Apocalypse.

'I have a wife. So does Lombard. We've got kids. So we're trying to hang on, for them.

'The other day Van Damme sent us telegrams saying Lecocq had killed himself, and he told us to meet.

'We were all together when you turned up. After you left, we learned that you were the one who now had the bloodstained suit, and that you were determined to track down the truth.'

'Who stole one of my suitcases at Gare du Nord?' Maigret asked, and it was Van Damme who answered.

'Janin. I'd arrived before you and was hiding on one of the station platforms.'

Everyone was exhausted. The candle end would probably last about another ten minutes, if that. The inspector accidentally knocked over the skull, which fell to the floor and seemed to be trying to bite it.

'Who wrote to me at the Hôtel du Chemin de Fer?'

'I did,' Lombard replied without looking up. 'Because of my little girl. My little daughter I haven't seen yet . . . But Van Damme suspected as much. Belloir, too. Both of them were waiting at the Café de la Bourse.'

'And it was you who fired the shot?'

'Yes . . . I couldn't take it any more. I wanted to live! Live! With my wife, my kids . . . So I was waiting for you outside. I've debts of 50,000 francs at the moment. Fifty thousand francs that Lecocq d'Arneville burned to ashes! But that's nothing – I'll pay the debts, I'll do whatever it takes, but to know that you were out there, hunting us . . .'

Maigret looked at Van Damme.

'And you were racing on ahead of me, trying to destroy the clues?'

No one spoke. The candle flame wavered . . . Lombard was the only one still illuminated, by a fading red gleam from the lantern.

It was then, for the first time, that Belloir's voice faltered.

'Ten years ago, right after the . . . the thing . . . I would have accepted my fate. I'd bought a revolver, in case anyone came to arrest me. But after ten years of living, striving, struggling! And with a wife and child now, well – I think I could have shoved you into the Marne myself. Or taken a shot at you that night outside the Café de la Bourse.

'Because in a month – not even that, in twenty-six days – the statute will be in force . . .'

Silence fell, and it was then that the candle suddenly flamed up and went out. They were left in utter darkness.

Maigret did not move. He knew that Lombard was standing at his left, Van Damme was leaning against the wall in front of him, with Belloir barely a step behind him.

He waited, without even bothering to slip his hand into the pocket holding his revolver. He definitely sensed that Belloir was trembling all over, even panting.

Maigret struck a match and said, 'Let's go, shall we?'

In the glimmer of the match, everyone's eyes seemed to shine especially brightly. The four of them brushed against one another in the doorway, and again on the stairs. Van Damme fell, because he'd forgotten that there was no handrail after the eighth step.

The carpenter's shop was closed. Through the curtains of one window, they could see an old woman knitting by the light of a small paraffin lamp.

'Was it along there?' asked Maigret, pointing to the roughly paved street leading to the embankment a hundred metres away, where a gas lamp was fixed to the corner of a wall.

'The Meuse had reached the third house,' Belloir replied. 'I had to wade into the water up to my knees to . . . so that he would go off with the current.'

Turning round, they walked back, passing the new church looming in the middle of vacant ground that was still bare and uneven dirt.

Suddenly they found themselves amid the bustle of passers-by, red and yellow trams, cars, shop windows.

To get to the centre of town they had to cross the Pont des Arches and heard the rushing river crashing noisily into the piers.

Back in Rue Hors-Château, people would be waiting for Jef Lombard: his men downstairs, amid their acid baths, their photoengraved plates waiting to be picked up by bicycle messengers; the new mother upstairs, with the sweet old mother-in-law and, nestled in the white bed sheets, the tiny girl who hadn't yet opened her eyes; the two older boys, trying not to make too much noise in the dining room decorated with hanged men.

And wasn't there another mother, in Rheims, giving her son a violin lesson, while the maid was polishing all the brass stair-rods and dusting the china pot holding the big green plant?

In Bremen, the commercial building was closing up for the day. The typist and two clerks were leaving their modern office, and when they turned off the electricity, the porcelain letters spelling *Joseph Van Damme, Import-Export Commission Agent* would vanish into the night.

Perhaps, in the brasseries alive with Viennese music, some businessman with a shaved head would remark, 'Huh! That Frenchman isn't here . . .'

In Rue Picpus, Madame Jeunet was selling a toothbrush, or a hundred grams of dried chamomile, its pale flowers crackling in their packet.

The little boy was doing his homework in the back of the shop.

The four men were walking along in step. A breeze had come up and was driving so many clouds through the sky that the bright moon shone through for only a few seconds at a time.

Did they have any idea where they were going?

When they passed in front of a busy café, a drunk staggered out.

'I'm due back in Paris!' Maigret announced, stopping abruptly.

And while the other three stood staring at him, not daring to speak and uncertain whether to rejoice or despair, he shoved his hands into his coat pockets.

'There are five kids at stake here . . .'

The men weren't even sure they'd heard him correctly, because Maigret had been muttering to himself through clenched teeth.

And the last they saw of him was his broad back in his black overcoat with the velvet collar, walking away.

'One in Rue Picpus, three in Rue Hors-Château, one in Rheims . . .'

In Rue Lepic, where he went after leaving the train station, the concierge told him, 'There's no point in going upstairs, Monsieur Janin isn't there. They thought he had bronchitis, but now that it's turned into pneumonia, they've taken him off to the hospital.'

So the inspector had himself driven to Quai des Orfèvres, where he found Sergeant Lucas phoning the owner of a bar that had racked up some violations.

'Did you get my letter, *vieux*?'

'It's all over? You figured it out?'

'Fat chance!'

It was one of Maigret's favourite expressions.

'They ran off? You know, that letter really had me

worried . . . I almost dashed up to Liège. Well, what was it? Anarchists? Counterfeiters? An international gang?'

'Kids,' he sighed.

And he tossed into his cupboard the suitcase containing what a German technician had called, in a long and detailed report, clothing B.

'Come along and have a beer, Lucas.'

'You don't look too happy . . .'

'Says who? There's nothing funnier than life, *vieux*! Well, are you coming?'

A few moments later, they were pushing through the revolving door of Brasserie Dauphine.

Lucas had seldom felt so anxious and bewildered. Skipping the beer, his companion put away six ersatz absinthes just about non-stop, which didn't prevent him from announcing in a fairly steady voice, and with only a slightly blurry and most unfamiliar look in his eye, 'You know, *vieux*, ten more cases like that one and I'll hand in my resignation. Because it would prove that there's a good old Good Lord up there who's decided to take up police work.'

When he called over the waiter, though, he did add, 'But don't you worry! There won't be ten like that one . . . So, what's new around the shop?'